Stone Chronicles: A piece of the past

Stone Chronicles, Volume 1

CheyScriv and Cheyenne Scrivens

Published by Cheyenne scrivens, 2024.

Also by CheyScriv

Stone Chronicles

Also by Cheyenne Scrivens

Stone Chronicles
Stone Chronicles: A piece of the past

Standalone
Town Full of Secrets

Prologue

<u>Xelle Stone</u>

I'm in too deep. "I don't know what to do," I exclaimed. "Ravi, you're bleeding out. What should I do?"

Coughing, he replied. "I'll be fine."

"No, you're not. You're losing too much blood. Let me call my sister for help."

He just nods.

With bloody hands, I pull out my phone out my purse and dialed my sister's number.

"Hello?" she answered.

"Khora, it's me. I need your help," I said, panicking.

"What is it now? Are you in jail again?"

"Khora…"

"You're in jail again, are you?"

"No, I'm not in jail. I'm being serious right now. I seriously need your help, Khora."

"What is it then?"

"Ravi was stabbed. He's bleeding out."

"Oh Ravi, is it? That boy has gotten you into trouble once again."

"Khora, please. Help us."

"No…"

"No?! What you mean no?"

"No, I won't help you. Ravi is always getting you into trouble. Let him get you two out of it. You're soiling our family's name by being associated with that thug."

Before I could reply, she hangs up. I looked over and Ravi was dead.

Chapter 1

<u>Lady hood/ Xelle</u>

"Congrats, everyone, on job well done," I praised my crew of friends, patting each one on the back.

"We couldn't have done it without you," a man said. All her crew agreed, celebrating.

Sorry, let me introduce myself. My name is Xelle Stone. My crew and I take from the wealthy and give to the under paid and overworked. A form of Robin Hood if you will. My crew and have been do this for some time now, two to three years. It was weird to be their leader at such a young age but I accepted it gracefully.

Currently, we are celebrating a job well done tonight. We perform... executed the plan perfectly. No casualties. No one was injured or killed. Thank God.

As everyone celebrated , my second and third of command and myself stored the money for safekeeping. We then returned to the celebration.

"Toast! Toast! Toast! Toast!" my crew chanted, pushing me towards the middle.

"Alright. Alright," I said, waving my hands to quiet everyone down. Once everyone was quiet, I began my speech. "We did a great job today," my crew began cheering again. I waved my hands again to quiet them and they quieted. "I'm proud to call you my friends. My brothers and sisters in crime. Please don't celebrate too hard. We have another job tomorrow," their cheering became louder. "But still celebrate," downing my drink. "Cheers!"

"Cheers!" my crew replied back.

I went to my chambers and began to undress when a knock sounded on my door. I quickly changed and answered it.

"Yes, who is it?" I asked.

"It's Lumin," my second replied.

"Enter," I said.

Lumin entered my chamber. "We need to talk," he said.

"About what?"

"This..." then pulled me into his arms and kissed me.

I pull back, breaking the kiss. "Lumin. Lumin, stop," while he began kissing my neck. "Lumin, stop," I moaned out. "Told... I told you, it's over. We have to stop."

"No, we don't. Just give in. You know you want to," he slid a hand into my pants and began rubbing me through my panties.

I leaned against him. I really shouldn't be doing this but it feels so good. I moaned. So so good.

"Fuck it," I gave in, going for his clothes. "This is the last time, Lumin."

"Sure. Okay," then he undressed me. "Sure."

Once we were both naked, Lumin enters me while I'm on my stomach. Making us both moan.

"Damn, I missed this," Lumin said beginning to move. He moved fast like they both liked.

"Ahh. Ahh," I moaned loudly. I move to all fours with my ass in the air.

Lumin holds my hips as he strokes into me. He moans along with me. He smacks my butt cheeks, making them jingle. Turning me on even more. My climax was building but I got there, Lumin pulls out. Nutting on ass as he moans my name.

"Xelle! Ahh! Xelle," he moaned loudly, he falls on the bed next to me.

I rolled my eyes and get up. I got to the bathroom to clean up. A minute later, I am dressed again. I notice Lumin was still naked on my bed sleep.

"Lumin. Lumin," I called. "Get up."

"Why? Is it morning?" he asked.

"Get out and go to your own chambers."

"Why? I'm comfortable here."

"I don't care. I want to sleep alone. Remember, it's over between us..."

"Shh," he said. "Come to bed."

"Either you go willingly or I'll force you, Lumin."

"Fine. Fine. I am leaving now," getting up and dressing. Once he was dressed, he walked to the door. "You're missing out on some great morning sex. Suit yourself," then shrugged and left.

When he was well enough away, I said, "Good riddens." I get into bed and finished myself off. I having sex with Lumin. It was always fruitless.

The next day, my crew and I gathered together so, I can brief them on our next target.

"Our target today is Dresden McKade. He is a billionaire. His company McKade Corporation," I informed them. "Lumin and Kyson, I want you to scope out the company. Kismet and I will be on surveillance. The rest of you get ready. We hit him and his company tonight. Everyone has their assignments. Let's go. Briefing over," then left.

Thirty minutes later, Kismet, Lumin, Kyson, and I went out and drove in separate cars, one of them a van. Kismet and I was in the van, Kismet was driving. Lumin drove the car.

Once we arrived at the McKade Corporation, Lumin and Kyson got out and went inside. Kismet parks the van down the street in the alley. We get out and get into the back.

"In the potion," Lumin said, acting like he was speaking into a cellphone.

"Alright. Go in," I said. "Don't give yourselves away."

"Yes, ma'am," the two men answered.

"Xelle, I have hacked into the McKade Corps main frame. Their firewall will take about five minutes to hack into the main systems," Kismet informed me.

"I'll help you cut the time down," I offered.

"Okay," she nods. "Thanks."

Another thirty minutes later, Kismet and I was in McKade's main system. We now control everything, from bank accounts to security systems.

Beep. Beep. Beep.

"Shit, somethings wrong," Kismet said, clicking on the keyboard.

"What? What happened?" I asked, concerned. I look over a Kismet's screens.

"We are about to be locked out and caught." I looked confused. "Someone at McKade Corp is changing the codes and passwords."

"So..."

"They're hacking us right now, Xelle."

"How?"

"The same as we are hacking them. Shit, we have two minutes to abort! We have enough..."

"Shit! Shit! Shit!" I cursed, before running my fingers through my hair.

<u>Dresden McKade</u>

"Sir, almost there," one of my hackers informed me.

"How much longer longer, Callen?" I asked , over their shoulder.

"About thirty seconds," he told me. "29. 28. 27. 26. 25..." he counted down.

"Send a virus to their computers, too." I ordered.

"Sir?"

"Just do it, Tej."

"Yes, sir," uncertain.

<u>Lady Hood/ Xelle</u>

"Damn it," Kismet cursed.

"What?" I demanded.

"They're uploaded a virus."

"What kind of virus, are we talkin' about?"

"One that will destroy our computer systems for good. We need to abort, Xelle."

I thought a moment. "Abort," I said defeated.

"Alright. Lumin and Kyson , Xelle said to abort mission," she told my crew through their communication links."

"Why?"Lumin demanded.

"Just abort, abort damn it!" I yelled the ordered at him. "I'll brief you later."

"Okay. Okay," Lumin said.

I get into the driver's seat and drive us home to our complex.

<u>Dresden Mckade</u>

"Sir, we lost them," my hacker said.

"How?" I demanded.

"They left the systems before we could do anything, sir."

"Damn it!" I cursed.

<u>Lady Hood/ Xelle</u>

"Why did we have to abort?" Lumin asked Kismet and me.

"I will brief you once everyone gets here," I told him.

"No..." he said.

"No? No! You will be briefed with everyone else, Lumin." I said, firmly.

As my crew files into the briefing room, I mentally gather my thoughts. So, I can address everything with the mission. Why did everything go wrong? I asked myself. How did Mckade Corp techies detect us? I should have planned for this. Shit. I run my hand ruffly through my hair.

Once my crew arrived, I called the briefing to order. My crew quieted down as I began to speak.

"We had a problem when Kismet and I hacked into McKade Corp main frame. In the beginning, it was easy until they found us. They were trackers us and was about to send a virus to our computer. We were almost caught. That's why I aborted the mission," I informed my crew.

"We could have still went on with the mission, Xelle," Lumin countered.

"Lumin, we couldn't have still went on with the mission," Kismet chimed in. "This virus could have fried our systems. We would have to build another system or try to debug this one."

"Damn it," he swore.

"Now, you understand, Lumin," I said. He nods. "We need a new plan any ideas?"

Dresden McKade

"Can you trace their whereabouts?" I asked.

"Sir?" my hacker asked, confused.

"I will tell you later. Can you do it?" he nods. "Okay, do it."

"Right, tracing their location." They pressed a few buttons for about five minutes. "Got them, sir."

"Where?"

"Sector 17. Isn't that where..."

"Lady Hood is located. Yes, that's what where I heard, too," I added. "Thanks." Leaving after patting his hacker on the back.

"What are you going to do, sir?" calling out.

"You'll see."

Lady Hood/ Xelle

After the briefing, I grab a glass of wine. As I am sipping my wine, Seren found me. She had a man with her.

Confused. "Who is this and how did he get here?" I demanded, setting my glassing down.

"Elle, this is Keandre Knight," she introduced us. "He's a hacker. I witnessed first hand him hacking into a sophisticated main frame like McKade Corp."

I stared him up and down. Keandre Knight didn't look like hacker. He looks like someone that never touched a computer in his life.

"Are you sure you can hack a computer?" I asked him. "Because you don't look like one."

"Show me to a computer and I can hack it, ma'am," he told me, confidently.

"Don't can me ma'am. Can me Elle or Xelle. Ma'am is my mother who has disowned me," I told him.

"Alright, Xelle, you may call me Dre or Keandre," Keandre said smiling at me.

Damn, he has to be sexy, I thought. "Alright, Keandre." then to Seren. "Go get my laptop from..."

"I remember where it is, Elle," Seren said cutting me off. "I will be right back," then left.

"So, why do you want to join our cause?" I asked, picking up my glass of wine and taking a sip. Before putting it down again.

"I want to join 'cause I'm tired of the rich having all the fun. I never fit in and o was hoping to fit in with you and your crew," he told me.

I asked Keandre two more questions before Seren came with my laptop with Lumin following behind her. Damn it, I cursed. What is he doing here?

"Thank you, Seren," I thanked her. Then to Lumin as I took my laptop from Seren. "What are doing here, Lumin?"

"What a random doing here?" Lumin countered. "How did he even get here? It's a secure location."

"I brought him here," Seren piped up. "We need a high level hacker to help and Keandre is it, Lumin."

"He doesn't look like a hacker. He looks like he never hacked anything in his life."

"Before you interrupted, Keandre was going to show us his skills," I told Lumin. He want to be in charge so bad. He is still trying to control me and the situation. I need do that quickly before everything gets out of control. "Lumin, I need to speak with you later," handing the laptop to Keandre.

Keandre set the laptop on the table on the other side of my glass of wine. I stand behind him. Seren was standing next to me.

"You have thirty minutes to hack Family National Bank," I told him. I look at watch. "Start...Now."

<u>Dresden McKade</u>

I pressed a few buttons on the laptop keyboard. It takes me around fifteen minutes to hack into the banks main systems. At the end, I'm a little detracted be Xelle's perfume. It was intoxicating and so was she. I mentally shake my head. Stick to the mission, Dresden. She's be your boss. You're here to take her and her bandits down.

"Done," I said.

"Impressive, Keandre," Xelle praised. "You're in."

"Elle, I don't think... something doesn't feel right," the man, Lumin protested.

"Lumin, walk with me. Talk with me," she said. Before leaving, she turned to Seren. "Show Keandre around and where he is staying," then left.

"Come with me," Seren said, leading the way. Leaving me to follow.

Chapter 2

<u>Lady Hood/ Xelle</u>

I'm currently in my chambers getting ready for bed when someone knocks on my door.

"What?!" I demanded, walking to my door. I grabbed my robe.

"Xelle, may I speak with you?" Keandre requested.

I close my robe tight before opening the door. I opened it to a half dressed Keandre. Damn, the sexiness, I groaned mentally.

"Can I help you with something" I asked.

"Yes, you can," he said and walked in to kiss me.

Startled, I pulled back. "What are you doing?" I groaned out.

"What I have been wanting to do since I got here and seen you," then he pulls me into another kiss.

Keandre walks me to my bed. He laid me down on it. He undid my robe and lifts my gown over my hips.

"Mmm," I moaned loudly. I moaned so, I woke myself up.

I sat up. Now, I'm wide wake somewhere scared to fall sleep. I get up then grab my robe and put it one over my gown. I leave my chambers then head to the break area kitchen to get something to drink.

I was startled when I saw Keandre sitting there. My dream came flooding back to me.

"What are you doing up?" I asked him.

Keandre cleared his throat. "I couldn't sleep. You?"

"The same. I had a weird dream," I replied.

"Care to share?" he asked.

"No, I'm okay," I lied. Why would I tell you when you're in it, I thought. I sip my water.

"Are you sure?" he asked, looking at me closely.

I nearly choke. "I'm sure," I reassured him. Damn, I hope I'm not making a mistake, I then thought. "I'm going back to bed. Goodnight, Keandre." Definitely making a huge mistake, I thought.

<u>Dresden McKade/ Keandre</u>

"Night, Xelle," I said back. She leaves.

Once she was gone, I groan thinking of what I really wanted to do with her. The dream I had of us came rushing back. I wanted to pull back or follow her to her chambers and fuck her senseless. Until we both can't move. Damn, I'm getting hard just thinking about it.

Thank God, no one is up but me, I then thought. I spoke too soon when Lumin walks in.

"What are you doing up, Knight?" he asked, going to get cup of something to drink.

"Couldn't sleep. Weird dream," I said, using the same words as Xelle used earlier.

"I see," he said. "Let's get one thing straight, Knight. Xelle's mine."

"You're telling me this why?"

"I don't like you or trust you. Once I find out why you're really here, I will you out personally. Get me, Knight?"

"Yeah, I do but let me tell you something; if Xelle wants me here, I'm here. If she wants me gone, I'll leave without your help. Seeing how she needs my help, I'll stay, Lumin," I retorted. "Xelle is her own woman. She can have anyone she wants," I added then got up and left.

In the hallway outside of the break room, Kismet stood. When she seen me, she looks at me eyebrows raised.

"What was that about?" Kismet asked.

"Nothing," I lied. "Night," leaving.

<u>Lady Hood/ Xelle</u>

The next morning, I noticed tension between Keandre and Lumin was more than usual. What happened between this? I wondered. Actually, I don't care.

"Keandre, can I speak with you a moment? Please?" I requested.

"Sure," Keandre replied, getting up and walks over to me.

Lumin gets up and followed him.

"Lumin, not you," I said. "Just Keandre."

He gets angry but doesn't go against my wishes. Good, I thought. But I will be getting cursed out by Lumin later. Great.

"Follow me," I requested, leaving.

Leaving with me, Keandre was following me down the hallway. I unlock my office and open the door. I hold the door open for him to walk inside. Once he was inside, I went inside and closed the door.

I walked over to my desk and sit behind it. "Have a seat, Keandre.

He sat in the chair across from me. "What do you want to talk to me about?" he asked.

I fold my hands together. "I want to get to know more about you. How did you become such a great hacker?" I asked.

"Well..." he began his story.

<u>Lumin</u>

Why did Xelle want to see Knight by herself? I wondered. I'm here second. Why can't I be present. Unless... Unless, she is trying to replace me. Oooh, that Bitch. She'd dare place me. After all I did for her, I'll show her. I make ideas to dethrone Lady Hood.

<u>Dresden McKade/ Keandre</u>

I told Xelle my story but omit I'm a billionaire. I also didn't tell her I own my own business. I told her the main basic things about myself.

After I was I done, she nods her head in approval. She types on her computer keyboard. She then turns the screen towards me.

"Is this you?" she asked.

I looked at the screen. She's good, I thought. But I was relieved to see the fake profile I set up. "Yes, that's me," I lied through me teeth.

Xelle node again. Before she could speak again, someone busted in the office.

"Elle, we have a problem!" a woman exclaimed.

"What it is, Kismet?" Xelle asked.

"Lumin starting trouble. Starting to get the crew against you," Kismet informed her.

"Again?!" she exclaimed.

"Yes, again, Elle."

"Why would he do that?" I wondered.

"He wants to dethrone me, Keandre," Xelle answered. "He wants to be in charge."

"I don't understand. Why does he want to be in charge?" I asked, confused.

"Because of you this time, I suppose," Kismet replied.

"Me? This time?"

"Yes, he thinks I'm replacing him, again," Xelle replied.

"Again? So, Lumin has felt this way before."

"Yes, he has." I'll have to straighten things out or just take his job. Hm, I'll do the second.

Lady Hood/ Xelle

Shit, I cursed. Lumin is making problems for again. I groaned in frustration. I really should kick him out but he knows too much. Shit, what am I going to do?

I call a private meeting, excluding Lumin, a few days later. There was Kismet, Kyson, and myself. I thought about inviting Keandre but he's too new to be present.

I had Kali and Scottie guard outside my office door to stop anyone from entering, especially Lumin.

Kyson sat in one of the seats across from my desk, next to Kismet, smoking a mini cigar.

"Will you put that out it?" Kismet complained. "It stinks, Ky."

He just continued smoking. Ignoring her, he asked, "Why are we having a meeting without Lumin?"

"Lumin is at it again. All because he thinks I'm replacing him," I replied. "Actually, I'm thinking of do just that..."

"Xelle..." Kismet started.

"No. No, Lumin is abusing his power and rank. I can't have him doing that anymore. He's using the crew including me to farther his agenda," I cut her off.

"So, what's the plan, Elle?" Kyson asked, blowing out a stream of smoke into the air.

"Keep an eye on Lumin. Report back to me with everything he does but don't breathe a word to anyone including him about what we're doing. Okay?" When Kismet and Kyson nodded, I said. "Okay. Meeting over."

As they were leaving, I pull the keyboard towards me. I look up Lumin's information. I look it over. Why did I pick him to be apart of my crew? Let alone be one of my closest friends. I really to reevaluate my crew members. I then I looked Keandre's information. I began to think over story. Maybe after sometime, Keandre might be willing to become a our hacker permanently.

<u>Dresden McKade/ Keandre</u>

I have been with Xelle and her crew for a few months now. I'm one of the three main hackers, includes Kismet, Xelle, and myself. I went on a few missions before but was always in the van with Xelle.

Currently, we're on on a mission. I'm the van hacking. Controlling the cameras, elevators, and the main frame. Xelle is hacking into their bank and off-shore accounts. She's sending the money somewhere. I can't see where. So that's how it's done. Hm.

"I think we're done here. Don't you think, Keandre?" she asked me. I just nod. "Okay. Call them out will you."

This is the first time Xelle asked me to do this. "Kismet. Lumin, we're all set. You can leave now," I said into the microphone for the comm links.

"Alright," Kismet answered.

"Yeah," Lumin replied.

Once Lumin, Kismet, Xelle, and I were back home. Xelle called a for a briefing. Lumin just ignored her orders and went somewhere in the opposite direction.

<u>Lumin</u>

Why should I go to the briefing? I was there, wasn't I? I can't believe Xelle is letting the new guy Knight call point. That's my job or Kismet's when we're on a mission. Not the new guy. I have to get dirt on him to get him kicked out with that bitch Xelle.

Lady Hood/ Xelle

That night, a few of the crew members and I was watching a broadcast about the jobs we placed in the last few weeks.

"Lady Hood and her crew has struck again. Stealing trillions from several companies and corporations. No one knows how they're doing it. All I have to say is..."

Someone shut off the broadcast before we got to hear the rest of it. I look over and see Lumin next to the television.

"Why are you watching this drivel?" Lumin demanded. "Don't you have beter things to do?"

I get and walk over to him. I shove him back then turn the television back on. "What's it to you?" I retorted. "Just because you're angry at me, doesn't mean you can take it out on everyone else, Lumin."

"No. Aren't you supposed to find us another mission for us? What you doing, huh?! Watching television!"

"Lumin, let's not do this here..." I tried to be reasonable. "Let's speak in private."

"No, I want to talk here," he countered.

"Come on, Lumin. Don't start here," one of my crew members said to him. "We're all winding down. Relaxing. Why can't you do the same? Leaving Elle alone, will you."

"Shut the fuck up, Reece! Who asked you?" Lumin replied to him.

"Enough, Lumin!" Kyson said fed up with Lumin's bullshit. "Come on, leave her be, man."

"Why is she even in change? She isn't even..."

He was cut off by two guards. They grab him.

"Take him the a holding cell," I ordered. "Thanks guys."

"No problem, Elle," one of the guards said.

Once Lumin was put in his cell, I went to my chambers to get ready for bed. As I was walking there, Keandre caught up with me. He had two glasses of wine in hand.

"Let's have a drink and forget what happened. Okay?" Keandre suggested, holding out the glass to me.

I thought a minute before nodding. "Okay," taking the glass.

"Would you like some company?" he then asked.

I was hesitant to answer. "You don't have if you don't wasn't to," he then said.

"It isn't that I don't want to, it's just…" I began.

"You don't want to make new rumors, right?" I nodded. "We're just two friends drinking together. We could go to the private common rooms since everyone is either sleep or watching tv."

Dresden McKade/ Keandre

I patiently waited for Xelle to reply. I know I am supposed to get dirt on her but... I don't know. Maybe just maybe, Xelle dealing with Lumin made thing different. Just a little. I even felt bad for her. Just a little.

"Okay, we can drink in common area near my chambers," Xelle finally replied. "Follow me."

She walked away leaving me to follow.

We went past a few doors to get to the common area Xelle was talking about. Once there, we went inside. She closed the door, also to I guess to have more privacy.

We sit on the couch near the TV. Neither of us turned it on. We just sat there together inn silence drinking our wine.

Chapter 3

<u>Lady Hood/ Xelle</u>

The next morning, I snuggled up to my pillow. I peeked an eye open and realized I wasn't in my chambers but still in the common area. And what I thought was my pillow, it was really Keandre. Shit, I jump up and away from him. That makes him stir awake.

"Morning," Keandre yawned, stretching.

"Morning," I said back.

"Oh wow," he said.

"What?" I said, waiting for his next words.

"I never so good in my life."

"What do you mean?"

"For year, I always had a hard time sleeping. Especially, recently..."

"You haven't, why?"

"Long story. I might tell one day."

"Another mystery to add to the list of Keandre."

"I told you in my interview all you needed to know about me, Xelle."

"Okay," He will never know my past, I thought. Never, say never, I then thought. My slogan coming back to haunt me.

I never told anyone this but I was rich or I come from a family. I left the family because no one would help me when I needed it. I would hangout with the hacks. They felt more like family than my own. That when I met my deceased fiancee, Kismet, and her brother Lumin, the dick. We been friends ever since. Anyway, my parents found out and they stopped helping me. Saying that Stones don't associate with those type of people.

"Elle, are you okay?" Keandre asked.

"Yes, why?" I replied.

"I asked you a question and you didn't reply," he said.

"Sorry, what was the question?" I apologized, sitting down on the far end the couch.

"I was asking how did you sleep?"

"I-I-I slept great, like a baby."

"A drooling baby," looking down at his shirt.

I look also. There was a small wet spot on his shirt on the chest area. I blushed for the first time in a long time. "Sorry about that," I apologized again.

"Stop apologizing. I should have insisted you go to your chambers but you were sleep so peacefully."

"Thank you for letting me sleep. I don't well either."

"That's why I saw you the first night I was here."

"Yeah."

"I have a question. Feel free not to answer it."

"Alright."

"What's up with you and Lumin? I have feeling he's more than your second."

"You're right. Lumin was indeed more than my second. He was supposed to be dating but I broke it off. He was using me to farther his own agendas."

"What was that?"

"To take over the crew and all the money for himself."

Why am I telling Keandre all this? I asked myself. Why am I revealing so much about Lumin and myself?

<u>Dresden McKade/ Keandre</u>

I can't believe that Xelle told me so much about her and Lumin. Now, I understand his disdain for me.

Xelle seems like she has been through a lot with Lumin. More than she's telling me. She might have gone through a lot at home life, also. She never spoke about her family when I first was interviewed.

"So, what about your family, Xelle?" I wondered.

"What about them?" Xelle countered.

"You never speak about them. Does your family or parents, more like, know what you're doing?"

"Why are you so interested in my family? What are you the blue suits?" she asked, being defensive.

"No, I'm not. I was just wondering..."

Before she could reply, someone opened the door.

"Elle, we have a problem," Seren told Xelle.

"What is it?" Xelle asked.

"I think..." she began looking at me.

"I'll give you ladies the room," I got up to leave.

As I walk to my chambers, I'm greeted by Kyson.

"Hey, bro," Kyson greeted me.

"Have you seen, Elle? She wasn't in her chambers."

"She should be with Seren in the private common area. Something happened..." I told him.

"Hey. Thanks, man," he said rushing off.

"No problem."

I continued to my way to my chamber. Once there, I shower and change my clothes. I went to the break area to get something to eat.

<u>Lumin</u>

I can't believe Xelle put me in the brig. She should have put that Knight guy here. How can she believe that wannabe? She's more gullible than I thought. When everything blows up in her face, I'll be there to clean everything up and be in charge.

<u>Lady Hood/ Xelle</u>

Ugh! I can't take it anymore, I groaned. Damn it! I cursed. Damn you Lumin. You got to go.

I went to the break area. I need a drink, I thought. I know it's early but I need one. I went the refrigerator to get a glass of wine. I take a long sip.

"Everything okay, Xelle?" Keandre asked.

I choke on the wine I was swallowing. I began to cough.

"Sorry to scare you, Xelle," he apologized, while patting my back.

Once I stopped coughing, I turned around and faced him. "That's okay. I shouldn't have been drinking like that. And to answer your earlier question; I'm not okay. I don't want to talk about it though."

"Alright. I'm here if need me...to talk that is."

"Thanks."

We sat in comfortable silence. Neither one of us spoke for while."

I continued to drink my wine. Keandre sits next to me drinking a water. Keandre breaks the silence.

"Xelle..." Keandre began.

Before I could respond, his phone goes off. He takes it and looks at the id. "I got to get this," he said, then apologized. "Sorry," then he sped off.

"Weird."

<u>Tej</u>

My boss has been undercover for months now. He usually calls with updates but he has not called in a few weeks so, I called him.

"Hello?" Mr. Mckade answered after two rings.

"Sir, do you have any progress?" I asked.

"Nothing I can tell as of yet. I'm still trying to get close to her," he replied. "I will call you once I know more," then he hung up.

<u>Dresden McKade/Keandre</u>

Tej had called me at the wrong moment. I was so close to having Xelle open up to me. Hopefully, no one heard me on the phone.

I walked out my room to see Seren. We look awkward at each other.

"Hey," I greeted her.

"Hello," she greeted me back. She then continued down the hall.

I walk back to the break area. Once I get there, I see Xelle fill her glass again. I also noticed her dosing off. She looked tipsy.

I rush in and take both the bottle and glass of wine away. "That's enough for you," I said.

"I'm fine, Keandre. I'm feeling good..." she said.

"You're drunk, Xelle," I corrected her. I helped her up. "Let's get you to bed, okay?"

"Okay but I'm not tired," falling asleep.

"Your eyes are closed, Boss," I jokingly told her.

Peeking one eye open. "So, I did," she giggles then she yawned.

"Let's get you in bed," I repeated.

I swept her up into my arms. I walked with her to her chambers. Once inside, I laid her on the bed. She doesn't let go. She is pulling me closer to her. Almost on top of her.

"Keandre, stay with me," she said.

I looked shock at her before lying next to her.

Lady Hood/ Xelle

I woke up with a headache. I tried to move but something stopping me. I tried to push the thing off me when it grunts. I pushed the thing again.

"Ouch, that hurts," the thing grunts.

I look over and see Keandre fully clothed next to me.

"What are you doing here, Keandre?" I demanded. "And in my bed."

"You were drunk. Falling asleep. I walked you to your chambers. You asked me to stay after I laid you in bed..." he recounted.

"Ugh, why do I have to tell you to stay?" I asked myself. Loudly enough for Keandre on accident. I looked over at him then groaned into my pillow. "Sorry."

"No, you okay," he yawned. "I'm going to go," getting up.

On instinct, I pulled Keandre back on the bed. I pulled him almost on top of me. He braced himself on his hands.

I looked up at him above me. I trace his face with my finger. I stopped at his lips. I looked into his eyes and he looked into mine.

As he leaned into kiss me, someone bursts into my chambers.

"Elle! Elle!" Kismet called me. She looked over at us on the bed. "Sorry. Am I interrupting something?"

Eruptly, Keandre and I pulled apart. I sat up as he rolled off me and stood up.

"No!" I exclaimed then cleared my throat. "Sorry but no you didn't interrupt anything. Keandre was just leaving."

He nodded then rushed out the room. Not looking at me or Kismet.

"Elle, really?!" Kismet scolded.

"What?!" I said.

"You and Keandre, really?" she scolded. "Have you not learned your lesson with Lumin?"

"I have but I think he will be different," I told her.

She looked long and hard at me. "Fine," giving in "Just be careful. Okay?"

"Okay," laying back down. "Shit, I need a drink."

"It's ten in the morning, Elle."

"It's five o'clock somewhere," rolling over and getting up.

Lumin

I can't believe Xelle is leaving me to rot in this cell. When I get out, she'll regret it. She better not be that 'Knight' guy. That pussy in mine.

Dresden McKade/ Keandre

I can't believe I almost kissed Xelle Stone. The notorious Lady Hood. I also can't believe I'm attracted to Xelle Stone. I'm a bachelor for a reason.

"Xelle's eyes are so beautiful and her lips..." I daydreamed. I cut off my sentence. "No. No. No. No, thinking about that. You're here for a reason . I need to stick to it," giving myself a pep talk. I made it back to my room and I heard my phone ringing.

"Hello?" I answered.

"Oh, honey, where have you been?" a woman asked.

"Krishna, how did you get this number?" I asked in a dead voice.

"Dres, don't be like that and your sister gave me this number. You know your family loves me. They want us to marry. Why won't just marrying? I'm your best match," Krishna pushed.

"I don't want to marry, ever. Please understand, I don't see myself with anyone."

"Never say never , Dresden. I could change your mind if you'd let me."

"I have to go. I have an important meeting in a few minute. Bye and lose this number," then I hung up with her still talking and calling my name.

I shut off the phone and change the sim card. I then change number. Hopefully, no one will get this number.

<u>Lady Hood/ Xelle</u>

I walked to the break area for breakfast. Once inside, I get a banana and a bowl of cereal. I went to sit at a table.

As I began to eat, Keandre walked in with a slight attitude. It wasn't pointed at anyone in particular. Just whoever was in the way.

Who made him get in that attitude that quickly?" I asked myself. In such a short bit of time.

I noticed him walking toward my table. He sat in front of me.

"Everything alright, Keandre?" I wondered.

"Peachy. Just peachy," Keandre replied.

"Want to talk about it?" I then asked.

"No, I don't," he replied.

"Okay," I said. "I think we need to talk about what happened earlier," I whispered to him.

"What is there to speak about, Xelle?" he demanded. "Nothing happened."

"Keandre, we almost…"

"Did nothing. So, drop it," harshly.

"Fine," being dismissive. I got up and left.

Chapter 4

<u>Lady Hood/ Xelle</u>

I walked back to my chambers to change. I thought since it's the weekend and I didn't make any missions, I'll let my crew and I relax. We haven't had any time off in a while. A few of my crew and I decided to go clubbing. So it's Seren, Kismet, Kyson, myself, and a few others. We head out and I notice Keandre is no where to be seen. My heart drops a bit before Kismet cheers me up.

We walked into Club Drama Circus. They carded us at the door before we were let in. There wasn't a cover fee since we were regulars. My crew and I were well known.

We went straight to our VIP section and ordered some drinks. Seren and Kyson got up to dance while the rest of us just sat enjoying the music. A cute guy comes over and talks to me.

"Hey beautiful, would you like to dance?" he asked me.

I thought a moment then I got up to join him. Anything to keep my thoughts off of Keandre, I thought. "Sure," I said, joining him on the dance floor.

We're dancing and he leaned in. "Name's Ezra and yours?" Ezra introduced himself.

"Xelle. My name is Xelle," I introduced myself.

"As in Lady Hood?" he asked.

"Yes," Here we go, I thought.

"That's..."

My stomach began to drop.

"...awesome. I wish I could pull off the things you do."

"Really? It's nothing."

A fast song is played. I turned around and grind against him while dancing. He holding onto me. I was letting myself go when I'm pulled forward.

"What the hell do you think you're doing?" a man's voice exclaims.

I looked at the man and it was Keandre freaking Knight. Just great. "What do you want, Keandre?" I retorted.

"I find you grinding on some other man after..." he began.

"Nothing. Nothing happened as you said... make up your mind."

Keandre grabbed me and kissed me. "Say that was nothing, Xelle."

"You're the one that said nothing happened. Why do I have to convince you?" I asked, almost demanding.

"Because..."

"Because what?"

<u>Dresden McKade/ Keandre</u>

I didn't know why, I thought.

"Well?" Xelle asked.

I don't want you with anyone else, I realized. But I can't say that.

"Because... because...shit! Never mind, then I eruptly let her go and left.

Damn it, I curse, walking straight the bar and ordering a scotch neat. I downed the first glass and sipped the next.

You want her, a small voice said. You want her in your bed tonight and want it to last forever.

No, I don't. I'm only here to her and her crew arrested for steal from my corporation. I'm not here to sleep with the enemy.

We'll see.

<u>Lady Hood/ Xelle</u>

I wonder what has gotten into Keandre then nerve to kiss me like that. He said nothing happened between us.

"What was that about?" Ezra wondered.

"Nothing," I lied. "It's nothing," I further the lie.

"If it's nothing then why is he drilling his eyes at us," he asked.

"Just ignore him."

"No can do. He is on his way back over here," he said. "I'll go before he..." he didn't finish his sentence and just left.

Just great, I thought. I began to walk back to the VIP section. When I'm stopping by Keandre.

"Let's dance," Keandre said.

A slow song plays.

"I'll sit the one out," I said.

"Please," was all he said.

"Fine," I gave in.

Keandre wrapped his arms around me as I place mine around his neck. We slowly rock to the music. I felt like we were the only ones there. I laid my head on his chest as we rocked to the slow music.

<u>Ezra</u>

Damn it! I couldn't find out more about Lady Hood. My boss is going to have my head.

<u>Lady Hood/ Xelle</u>

Later that night, Keandre and I said goodnight to the others before he walked me to my chambers. Once outside of the door, I unlock the door and let myself inside but I didn't go in right away.

"Well, goodnight," Keandre said.

"You not coming in?" I asked, wondering.

"You want to come in?" he asked. He stands in my doorway.

"Yes, I do want you to come in," I replied, taking his hand and pulled him inside.

"Okay," walking forward inside,

I closed the door behind him. He kissed me as he backs me into my bed. He lets me crawled onto it. He doesn't join me and broke the kiss. He just stares at me.

"Are you sure?" Keandre asked. "There's no going back." I answer by undressing and pulling him onto of me.

We began kissing as he climbed between my legs. He was still fully clothed.

As he began kissing my neck, I say, "You have too many clothes on, Dre."

Keandre backed off the bed and undressed then climbed back between my legs. He kissed down my body until he was between my thighs. He leans in and sucked on my clit. I gasped at the feeling because it was so foreign. Lumin never done this before. Shit, Lumin . I forgot he was in the brig.

Keandre must have noticed I wasn't focused on him. He began fingering me as he sucked on my clit. I gasped against and lost all train of thought.

"Aahh," I moaned, squirming under his mouth and hands.

<u>Dresden McKade/ Keandre</u>

Her moans was making me hard just hearing them. I felt her close around my fingers when she climaxed. I moved back up her body. I positioned myself between her leg then entered her.

"Mm," we both moaned.

Damn, so good. So good, I thought.

I began moving and Xelle continued moaning. I moved a little faster, making her moan even more.

"Yes! Right there!" Xelle moaned aloud. "Right there!"

She moaned my name as she climaxed hard, creaming on my shaft. I continued to move sending her towards her climax again, making her scream in pleasure, I finally climax and fall next to her.

Lady Hood/ Xelle

That was best I had in a long time. Keandre just...wow. He gave me three orgasms before his own. Unless like...damn. Damn, I thought.

I felt his arms wrap around me then heard his even breathing. Thinking he was sleep I turn to face him. He had his eyes closed. I began to trace his face when his eyes opened and looked at me.

"Hey, what are you doing?" Keandre asked.

"I-I-I..." I stuttered. I never stutter. What has come over me? I questioned myself. What's wrong with me?

"Never mind," he said. "Let's just go to sleep. We have plans."

"What sort of plans?" I asked.

"You'll see," then he closed his eyes again.

Tej

It was been while since I heard from Mr. McKade. I might have to call in reinforcements. I know he won't like it but...

<u>Lumin</u>

That bitch! I can't believe her. She's mine. Xelle Stone is mine, I thought. When the guards was talking about last night. I listened and overheard them about Xelle and Knight together. Dancing and shit. They better hadn't... I thought. Deep down inside he knew they did.

Wait until I get out of here. If I get... no, when I get out of here, I come for them. "I'm coming for Xelle Stone and Keandre Knight," I said loud then began to laugh, evil.

<u>Kismet</u>

Damn, Xelle is with Keandre. Good for her. I get up for the day hungover. I have a splitting headache. I look for my painkillers. Once I find them, I took two.

My headache was gone by the time I left my chambers. I meet up with Xelle. She was in the break area, getting coffee.

"So...how was your night?" I asked Xelle.

She jumps and I chuckled. "Hey, it was good," she replied, not giving anything away.

"You and Keandre...spill." When she doesn't say anything and kept her face neutral, I pushed. "Come on. Tell me. Tell me. Please."

I then was pulled into the hall and down into the private common areas. Xelle then locked the door.

<u>Lady Hood/ Xelle</u>

I can't believe Kismet is assuming Keandre and I did something last night. Don't get it twisted, something did happen but I didn't want everyone in the crew to know it.

"Xelle..." Kismet called.

"Something did happen with Keandre," I confessed.

"No! Noooo! No way!" she exclaimed.

"What?" I asked. "I didn't finish..."

"You two did it? You two did it!" she questioned then exclaimed.

"Shh, someone might hear you."

"Wait, I'm right!"

"Shh. I'm not going to say anything unless you..."

"Sorry," in her normal voice. "Continue. Continue."

"Thank you," I said. "Yes..." I wait for Kismet to speak again. When she didn't, I continued. "Yes, I did it with Keandre..."

"I knew it! I knew it!" then I just gave her look. "Sorry. How was it?"

"Really?!"

"What?"

"You're really asking me that?"

"What? It wasn't good was it? I'm sorry, Elle."

Grinning. "It was great. Just great."

Smiling. "Details. Details."

"Well..."

Dresden McKade/ Keandre

I was whistling as I walking into the break area. Everyone became quiet, staring at me.

"As you were," a woman's voice said from behind me.

I turned around and saw Xelle and Kismet walking in. I smiled and walked over to them. Once I wasnear them, Kismet excused herself then walked away.

"Morning, Xelle," I said.

"Morning, Keandre," she said.

We walked to the buffet of food. She grabbed a muffin and a piece of fruit. I grabbed a plate and filled it up with food. We went to an empty table and sat down,

Everyone was still staring at us. It making me uncomfortable.

"Stop staring!" she yelled the order. 'As you all were!"

Everyone stopped staring and went back to what they were doing. I sighed in relief. She looked beautiful, I thought.

Lady Hood/ Xelle

After everyone stopped staring at Keandre and me, I knew everyone was curious about us. Even after last night, I'm not surprised when Kismet cornered me earlier. Asking me what happened and details. Damn, here we go, I groaned inwardly.

Chapter 5

<u>Lumin</u>

I'm finally out the brig. That bitch forgot about me. I walked in the break area after a much needed shower. When I walked inside I saw Knight and Xelle sitting together. Before I could storm over to them, I'm stopped by Kyson.

"Not here. Not now, Lumin," Kyson said to me. I tried to push pass him but he wouldn't let me. "Not here. Not now," he repeated.

I then nodded in agreement before leaving, I looked back at them.

<u>Dresden McKade/ Keandre</u>

As I face away from the doorway, I felt someone's eyes on Xelle and me. I turned back just in time to see Lumin's retreating back. I turned back and noticed Xelle didn't see him. I'm happy because we don't have anymore drama than we are already caused today. Xelle looks over at me with a question on her face.

"You okay?" she asked me.

"I'm fine, why?" I replied.

"I called you and you didn't respond."

"Sorry, I..."

"You saw Lumin."

"You let him out," it was a question but a statement.

"Yeah, I couldn't just leave him there..."

<u>Lady Hood/ Xelle</u>

I could have actually left him there but I needed to keep a watchful eye on Lumin. Personally, I wish I could kick him out before he could get a chance to do anything to Keandre or myself. I'm tired of Lumin's bullshit. I'm about tired of him pouting or arguing when he can't get his way.

The son of a bitch was going to confront us because he was mad. The asshole made his bed now, he needed to lay in it.

"Everything will be okay, Keandre," I lied. Wholeheartedly, I thought trouble is just beneath the surface with Lumin. Shit, here we go.

"Just be careful around him, okay?" Keandre requested.

"I will. You too, okay?" I requested back. He nods. "I'm planning to do something about Lumin. I promise you." Keandre just nods again then gets up to leave.

"I need to prepare for the next mission," he said. He then left.

"What was that all about?" Kismet asked, coming to sit with me.

I saw her sit in Keandre's vacant seat. "I think Keandre is upset because I let Lumin out of the brig."

"What?!" she exclaimed. "You let him out. Why?"

"I can't let Lumin rot in the brig."

"I would have after what he did and going to do."

"I can't leave him there for something he's going to do, Kismet."

"I can't deal with you," she was about to get up and leave.

"Wait," I said.

"Why?" Kismet demanded.

Before I could reply, one of my crew walked over to us. "Elle, everything is all set for the briefing."

"Thank you, I'll be right there," I told them.

"We have a mission?" Kismet asked as the man left.

"Yes, there is," I confirmed. "Let's go then." Getting up and walking out of break area. Leaving Kismet to follow.

<u>Dresden McKade/ Keandre</u>

I can't believe Xelle let Lumin out the brig. She may have a bigger problem than she realized. I know that she had a plan but...

Before I could finish, my phone rang. It was puzzling because no one should have this number but Tej. I told him to waiti for more information. So, who was it?

"Hello?" I answered the phone.

"Hey, son," the man greeted me.

"How did you get this number?" I demanded. "No one should have it."

"I have my ways, Dresden," my father told me.

"Why are you calling me? I'm busy, Father."

"You haven't been update Tej about your plans going forward."

"I'm still gathering intel, Father. I need to go. Someone might come looking for me. I can't be caught talking to go. I promise to call with more intel..."

"But you had several months to do so, what's the hold up, son?"

I was not going to tell him that I had feelings for Lay Hood. "Like said I'm gathering more intel," I repeated the lie. Trying to convince my father and myself that is what I should be doing.

At that moment, someone knocked on my door. "Keandre, it's time for the briefing," they said then walked away.

"Father, I need to go," I said. "I'll call soon," then hung up before kept me on the phone longer.

I put the phone away and went to the briefing.

Kismet

Now that Lumin was out of the brig, there would be trouble coming. It would get worse, also.

Lady Hood/ Xelle

Keandre has been acting weird around me. Lumin has been eyeing me with an evil eye. Everyone else was uneasy with the tension in the room.

I called the room to order. I brief my crew on the mission we were doing. I appointed Keandre, Kismet, and Kyson to join me. I left everyone else, including Lumin, at the base. I looked briefly at him and noticed he was unset. Angry to be exact. I just ignored it. The briefing was over. As my crew dispersed and left the briefing room. Only people that were left was Kismet, Keandre, Kyson, and myself.

"Are you sure about this, Elle?" Kyson asked me what everyone was thinking.

"I'm sure, Kyson," I replied. "I'm not dealing with...Not now... Change and lets get going."

Lumin

Damn Xelle. She lets boy-toy be on the mission and not me. Damn her. She will regret it. That she will.

<u>Kismet</u>

The tension was horrible earlier. I can't believe Xelle even let Lumin out the brig. She should have let him rot. That's what I would have done. Now, we have to deal with Lumin and his bullshit. Why? Oh, why do we have to deal with the tension. Next time, I wish she would have let him rot.

Lady Hood/ Xelle

While I was changing and packed my book-bag, a knock sounded on my door. I knew who was knocking from the sound. Mother fucking Lumin was at my door. Son of a... Please not now.

Lumin continued to knock. I was still regretting letting him out. I knew he was confronted me about earlier but I don't have time for time. Let's get this over with, I thought as I opened the door.

I opened the door to an angry Lumin standing there. "May I help you?" I asked as civil as I can.

"You can help me by putting on the mission, Xelle," Lumin said, walking into my chambers.

"Alright, you can come in," I said sarcastically.

"Xelle, cut the shit. Why didn't you put me on this mission?" he demanded.

"Lumin, you just got out the brig. I can't just you down a mission. You know the rules," I exclaimed.

"Well, screw the rules, Xelle. They're bogus and you know it. Otherwise, your boy-toy would be still surveillanced and looked into.

"Keandre isn't my boy-toy."

"Then you must be his whore."

"Lumin! Please leave..."

"Not until I get what's mine," as he walked toward me.

Lumin shoved me on the bed then gets on top of me. I tried to push him over but he is too strong. He held me down. I still continued to try and push him off me. He grabbed my hands in one hand and my hair in the other. He tries to kiss me but before he could, a knock sounded on my door.

"Whoever, it is go away. Xelle is busy!" Lumin yelled the command.

"Elle, are you okay?" a woman's voice, I now know as Kismet, demanded.

"Tell her you're fine," he whispered the command. He looked like he had something planned if I didn't. "Tell her," he repeated.

With a shaky voice, I replied. "I'm fine, Kismet. Just meet me at the van."

"Are you sure?" she asked.

"Yes, now go," I reassured her. Hoping she would take the hint and get some help. She knows I like to walk with her to the van.

"Okay," then I heard Kismet's footsteps retreat.

"Now...where were we?" Lumin sneered.

I now regretted letting Lumin out the brig.

<u>Kismet</u>

I sped up the pace to find someone to help Xelle. Lumin planned on doing something to her. As I raced down the hallway, my face looked scared and panicked.

Keandre or Kyson. I must find them. I tried looking everywhere for them. I don't see them anywhere. I then remembered we have a mission to do. I had totally forgot that quick. I raced to the garage and found them.

"Elle is in trouble!" I told them. "Lumin is with her. She sounded scared. Come quick!" then I raced back to Xelle's chambers.

"Damn you Lumin! You'll pay dearly," I exclaimed.

<u>Dresden McKade/ Keandre</u>

After Kismet told me what happened, my blood ran cold. Without a care of the equipment, I shoved it back in the van as I ran after Kismet.

On the way to Xelle's chambers, I signal for the guard to follow me. As they followed, one of them asked what happened.

"Lumin is what happened." was all I said. "Let's go," I then ordered.

Once at Xelle's door, I! banged on the door.

"Go away! We're busy!" Lumin yelled from inside.

I bang on the door again.

"Go away or you'll regret it!" he threatened.

At that moment, I decided to kick the door in. It slammed opened with a bam against the wall. I rush in with the guards. After we rushed in, we see Lumin holding Xelle down. Before I could get to them, the guards rushed in and tried to get him off her.

After Lumin was pulled off Xelle, I went to her and held her. She was shivering like she was cold but I knew she was scared.

"Take him to the brig. He isn't to be let out," I commanded, taking charge.

"You can't do that," Lumin said.

"But I can," Xelle retorted. "Give him the special treatment this time," she smirked. "Take him away."

Lumin was now struggling against the guards. "No! No! No!" he yelled. "Please no!" he pleaded.

Once Lumin was gone, there was only Xelle, Kismet, and myself left in Xelle's chambers. We were silent until Kismet clears her throat.

"Are you alright, Xelle?" Kismet asked.

Xelle nodded. "I'm fine now that you and Keandre saved me," she replied. "Thank you, I'm so grateful." She hugged Kismet then myself.

I noticed she held me longer. Kismet cleared her throat again.

"I'd better be going," Kismet said, walking to the door. "Question: Are we still down the mission?"

"Yes, I'm not going to let Lumin's scare me," Xelle replied, confidently.

I was both proud and concerned for her. "Are you we? We can put it off…"

"No, I'm alright now. I was shaken up before you and Kismet brought the guards. It's just sad it came to that extreme…"

"You knew Lumin was planning something, right?" I asked her.

"Yes, I knew but that was crazy."

"What was that about 'special treatment'? what's that?"

"Nothing to worry about that, Keandre. You haven't done anything to warrant that," dismissing me.

I gave up. "Kismet, I need to talk to Keandre alone for a moment then we'll be right behind you," Xelle requested.

"Okay," Kismet said, walking out the door. Leaving us alone.

<u>Lady Hood/ Xelle</u>

"Are you sure, you're okay?" Keandre asked, concerned.

Walking away from him and wrapped my arms around myself. "I'm fine. Really," I reassured him.

He continued to look concerned.

"Keandre, you and the crew members that recused me just in time," I told him. "Lumin didn't get to do anything to me."

"He better be happy he didn't," he said with venom in his voice.

"Calm down," I commanded, gently. "No need to get angry."

I saw him trying to calm down but the little I know about Keandre, he was stilling picturing the whole scene from earlier with Lumin. I instantly regretted it. I'm upset that everything happened. Also, that I let Lumin out the brig.

Chapter 6

<u>Lady Hood/ Xelle</u>

After the mission was a successful. Kyson, Kismet, Keandre, and I traveled back to our base to inform the rest of the crew. We were excited to tell everyone until we saw on of the guards waiting outside the complex.

We park and get out. There was concern and panic on their face. I walked up to them.

"What happened?" I demanded.

"Lumin..." the guard began.

"What about him?" I demanded, staring at him.

"L-L-Lumin escaped," he stuttered.

"Whattt?!" I exclaimed. "How is that... What?!"

"We're sorry," they apologized.

"Explain!" I commanded.

"We were taking Lumin to the brig when a few men overpowered us and he escaped."

"To where?"

"We don't know but we sent our scout after with a few blue coats, that are with our cause, after him. As we speak."

"Inform me when he is taken into custody. Do you I make myself clear?"

"Yes ma'am. I will tell the others," bowed then walked away.

"Damn you Lumin!!!" I exclaimed.

Lumin

Fuck you, Xelle!" I cursed. "You'll pay.

I ran to the hideout I built awhile back. I opened the door with my hidden key. I walked in and turn on the lights. I went and located my phone. After turning it on, I checked it.

Lady Hood/ Xelle

"Just great," I said, pacing in my office. I was with Kismet, Kyson, And Keandre. "I can't believe Lumin escaped. He had to be planning this."

"Probably," Kismet agreed. "It figures for my brother."

Kyson looked like he wanted to say something but I didn't.

Keandre must have noticed his face. "Ky, you know something, don't you?" he asked.

I look at Kyson as I stopped pacing briefly. "Do you know, Kyson?" I demanded, zeroing in on him.

"Tell me," I commanded.

He hesitated.

"Come on, Ky. Tell us," Kismet pushed. "You might as well."

"Yes. Yes, he planned it," Kyson gave in. "He planned a lot more than you know."

"Like what?" Keandre demanded.

"Wouldn't you like to know," he replied.

"Kyson, tell us," I commanded.

Kyson stayed quiet. He doesn't answer. He just left the room.

Kismet, Keandre, and I was shocked by Kyson leaving. Kismet followed him. We could heard them yelling at each other for five minutes before Kismet dragged Kyson back into my office.

"Kyson?" Kismet said. "Tell them," she then ordered.

"Damn it," he cursed. Before he could tell, someone busted in.

"Elle, we have a huge problem," a crew member exclaimed.

"Jesse, what happened now?" I asked.

"I went to gather the others. Some of them are gone. They're missing," Jesse told us.

"What?!" we exclaimed.
"They're gone, Elle," he replied.
"Must have been Lumin, Elle," Kismet said.

"I know that, Kismet but when did he get followers?" I wondered. I then turned to Kyson. "Kyson, spill!"

We all stared and waited for him to speak.

Lumin

I can't believe Lady Hood didn't realize that I had ass this planned as smart as she is, I have followers. She and her little boy-toy won't know what happened after I'm done with them. I laugh evilly.

Dresden McKade/ Keandre

That son of a bitch Lumin, I cursed. My plans are being changed because of that asshole. My father won't be pleased if there is any delay.

After Kyson told us everything, Xelle was visibly angry when she swiped everything off her desk. I knew she wanted to throw something because I wanted to, too.

"Damn it!" she cursed. "He had plans no matter what I did to him. That's son of a bitch."

I walked over to Xelle but she moved away from me.

"Keandre, don't," she said. "I don't want to hurt you."

"You won't hurt me. Come here, Xelle," I requested. I opened my arms to her.

She walked over to me and into my arms.

"Can you give us the room? Please?" I requested.

Kyson, Kismet, and Jesse nodded and exited the room. We were alone. Xelle, I knew, was very angry. So angry that I felt her tears soaked my shirt.

"Xelle…" I began.

"Keandre, don't," she said. "I knew some of the crew would and followed Lumin. I just didn't realize sooner."

"It was only a matter of time it would happen, Xelle. Lumin must have been planning this for a while now."

"I know but damn him," she cursed. I visibly see her bring herself together and calm herself. "I need to call a meeting. I need..." before she finish, I kissed her. "What was that for?" she asked.

I shrugged. "Just because."

She nods. "Okay," then kissed me again.

<u>Lady Hood/Xelle</u>

Keandre laid me down on the floor. "Is the door locked?" he asked as he began to undress me.

"We don't have time for this, Keandre," I moaned, letting him do it.

"Yes, we do. You need to..." he began.

Melting under his lips and hands. "Before you finish that sentence, I'm going to be fine. I knew this was going to happen," I said, cutting him off.

"I know you were prepared but the betrayal still hurts, Xelle."

Instead of letting the tears flow, I pulled at his pants and his cock sprang free. I hiked up my the skirt I was wearing and straddled him. He entered me and we moan. I began to move on him.

<u>Lumin</u>

A few the crew members met up with me at the hideout. They were glad they weren't under Xelle's rules any longer. They were tired as I was of her bullshit rules and never having anything.

"Lumin, hey bro," a man greeted me.

I recognize the man's voice. The voice came from my older brother, Quinlan."Hey, big bro," I greeted him back, embraced him. "When did you get here?"

"Not too long ago," Quinlan replied. "One of your crew members let me in. Also, you told me to get through anyway before you left."

"True," I agree. "I'm so happy I left the stupid bitch. Letting some random come in and take what's mine or have been mine for nine years."

"Well, I looked into your friend, Keandre Knight and..."

"Knight isn't my my friend, Quin!" I yelled. "What did you find out?"

Quinlan pulled out a folder out of of his jacket. Handing it to me, he began. "Keandre Knight's records is a mile long but there's nothing about any hacking crimes noted.

"There wasn't, eh?" I grinned sinfully.

"No," he confirmed. "What are you planning?"

"You'll see, Quin. You'll see," as I rubbed my hands together.

<u>Dresden McKade/ Keandre</u>

That son of a bitch is going to blow my cover. Shit!

"You alright, Xelle?" I asked.

"Mm. Hm," Xelle replied, sitting up. She was distant.

"Are you sure?" I asked, looking at her dress.

"Yes, I'm sure," she confirmed, putting her last piece of clothing on. Slipped on her shoes then walked to the door. "Let's go. Get ready. We're late," leaving her office closing the door.

Something is definitely wrong, I thought. Damn...Fuck you, Lumin.

<u>Lady Hood/ Xelle</u>

Damn that bastard Lumin, I cursed as I walked down the hall to my chambers. I shouldn't have done anything with either Keandre or Lumin. I need to leave them two alone. Permanently. Easier said than done.

I entered my chambers. I take a quick shower and dressed again. I left my chambers and went to the briefing room. I wanted to cry but I needed to be strong. I'm no weak minded person. I have a briefing to do and Lumin to deal with.

I coached myself on as I neared the briefing room. I walked in and saw a third of my crew was gone. Shit, I didn't think it would be that many with Lumin, I thought.

I walked to the front of the room. When they saw me, my crew quieted down.

"First order of business, Lumin is no longer with our crew. He escaped and took third of our crew with him."

"Good riddens," one of the crew members yelled.

"Yeah!" all the other crew yelled in agreement.

"Hey Elle, we are better with you anyway," Kismet yelled, then the crew yelled in agreement.

"Xelle! Xelle! Xelle!" Keandre chanted. I smiled at him as the rest of the crew chimed in, chanting.

After a few minutes, I quieted everyone down again.

"Alright. Alright," I yelled loud enough so everyone heard me. "Second order of business, we successfully pulled of the mission we did."

I noticed Keandre slip from the room. I make a mental note to talk to him again.

I finish the briefing and dismiss everyone. I walked out the briefing room to locate Keandre.

<u>Kismet</u>

Damn you, Lumin! Always putting us in a weird spot. Doing this mess and leaving Xelle to clean it up as usual. She now has so much on her plate because of them.

I watched Xelle follow Keandre out the room. He seemed to be off now. I can already tell it is because of Lumin.

"Damn you, Lumin."

Dresden McKade/ Keandre

I decided to leave the briefing because I already know everything that happened. I walked outside for some air. I took out a cigarette and my lighter. I tried lighting it and but the lighter wouldn't light. The click of the lighter, in front of me, caught my attention.

I took a drag then turned to see who lit it. It was Xelle. She took out her own cigarette and lit it. She then took a long drag. She blew out the smoke and sighed.

"Damn it!" Xelle cursed , loudly. She took another drag then blew it out.

"Are you alright, Xelle?" I asked, taking another drag.

Annoyed, she looks over at me. "I wish you would stop asking me that. I'm fine," she replied.

I saw the tears in her eyes. I pull her into my embrace. We held each other so long we lost track of time.

<u>Lumin</u>

I wondered how Xelle was fairing but only because I don't trust Keandre Knight. I would've stayed...Ha, wouldn't have stayed. Good riddens the both of them.

I needed to get my plan into motion. "Xelle Stone. Keandre Knight or whatever his name is. They're going to pay and they won't see it what happens.

<u>Scorpius Stone</u>

"Have you found her?" I demanded.

"No but I am close," my private investigator told me.

"How close are you?" I then demanded.

"Very close, sir," my private investigator replied.

"Your granddaughter, Ms. Stone just hit a company close to ours financing. They had poor security so everything or almost everything is gone.

"I see," I said, steeping my hands. I stared beyond him and think. Secretly, I was proud of my granddaughter. Her independence and work she has done still she been...

"Sir?" my assistant called, walking in my office.

"Hershey, what is it?" I asked.

"You have a meeting in thirty minutes, sir," Hershey replied.

"Okay, give me a minute or two."

He nodded then left.

I get up and dismiss my private investigator before leaving for my meeting.

Chapter 7

<u>Lady Hood/ Xelle</u>

I was waiting for Kismet to meet up and sign some papers for donations. A few minutes later, she came in my office and closed the door.

"Elle, I'm worried about you," Kismet concerned.

I sigh. "I'm fine, Kismet," I brush her off, going back to work looking over the papers.

She sighs and sat in the chair in front of my deck. "You've been working too hard, Elle," she comments. "Everyone is worried. You're snapping at everyone."

"I said I'm fine, Kismet," I said a little snippy.

"See... You're not fine. You usually don't snap at me or anyone like that."

I sigh loudly and putting my papers down again. I looked up at Kismet. My eyes swelling with tears.

"Aw honey," she said as she gets up and came around the desk then hugged me. "I knew something was up."

"Shh, don't say it so loud," I said. "I don't want anyone to know."

"Everyone already knew," she said. "You're too late."

Dresden McKade/ Keandre

I was worried about Xelle even though I shouldn't be. She have been evading me all this time since we had sex to comfort her. I kind of understand but I'm not even going on the missions she goes on.

Walking past Xelle's office, I heard her cries and Kismet soothing her. I don't know why I care. I have a mission of my own: Take Xelle and her crew by any means necessary. I can't get involved with her in anyway.

"Fuck it," I said to myself. I went in anyway. They didn't see first until I cleared my throat.

They looked over at me in the doorway. I noticed Xelle tensed when she saw me.

"What do you want, Keandre?" Xelle demanded.

"I was worried about you," I replied. "You have been avoiding me. I understand..."

"Keandre..." she began.

"I understand what with Lumin has upset you, even angered you but..."

"Keandre, not now. Maybe later. I can't deal with this right now."

"I agree with Elle, Dre," Kismet agreed.

"I know she is dealin' Kismet but I want in on the missions. I thought you said I was a great hacker."

"You are but..." Xelle began.

"No buts, Xelle," I countered. "Tell me why."

<u>Kismet</u>

I can't believe how selfish Keandre is. Just like a man. Ugh, I wish he would go away leave us be. I almost had her calmed down. Keandre just had to interfere. Ugh.

<u>Scorpius Stone</u>

"Grandfather, any news about Xelle?" my other granddaughter asked me. I know she resents me her sister for walking away from the family. Even though, we turned on her first. "Grandfather?"

"Oh sorry, my dear child," I apologized halfheartedly. "No new news about your sister, Khora."

"She isn't my sister, Grandfather. She is the who abandoned us for some boy," Khora retorted.

"Khora Stone, that isn't in any way right to say," I scolded.

"So?" she replied.

"So, that's your sister, you're speaking about."

"She isn't here. Why should I care then?"

"Xelle isn't here to defend herself, Khora. Watch your mouth young lady!" I ordered.

"Yes, Grandfather."

I know she lying by her voice. I need to find Xelle before something happens to me. I also that Khora could be crazy.

A knock sounded on the front door. The doorman answered it.

"Sir, a Mr. Lumin and Mr. Quinlan Drake here to see you," the doorman told me.

Lumin's here. Weird. Show them in, Franklin," I said.

Frankin walked back to the door and showed them in. "This way gentlemen," I heard him say from archway.

"Thank you, Franklin," I thanked him. "You may go," he nodded his head and left. "What can I do for you, gentlemen?"

"It's what can I do for you, Mr. Stone," Lumin said.

"What do you mean by that?" Khora demanded.

"Shush. The men are talking," he said.

"Excuse me?!" she exclaimed.

"Khora, please..." I chimed in.

"But.."

"Give us the room, child."

Khora storms off in a huff.

"Now, what have got to tell me, Lumin? After insulting my granddaughter," I demanded.

"Which granddaughter?" Lumin asked, smirked.

"What do you mean by that, Drake?" I countered.

"Your granddaughter, Xelle, I'm talking about, Mr. Stone," he replied, continuing to smirk.

"What about her?"

"I have news about her."

I looked him then Quinlan, who nodded.

<u>Lady Hood/ Xelle</u>

Weeks later, everything that happened wrong happened. My crew and messed up a mission and almost lost people to the blue suits. They somehow knew where we were going to be. Damn, whoever told the blue suits of our missions. Wait a minute...Lumin knows. He could've told our plans to the blue suits. May he rot in hell.

"Xelle, what happened out there?" Keandre asked me, walking next to me.

"I don't know, Dre!" I shouted. "And don't start in on me. Got it!" I stormed off.

<u>Dresden McKade/ Keandre</u>

Damn it, I cursed as I saw Xelle storm off. I understand she's stressed out but I want to know what happened. Hopefully, she'll brief everyone of what happened.

"Everyone report the briefing room for the debrief," Xelle announced over the speaker.

Maybe, I will get my answer. I walked towards the briefing room.

Twenty minutes later, the crew, that was left, was in the briefing room. I stood to the side with some of the others as Xelle told us what happened today.

"I know many of you are wondered what happened today. Well, I don't know or understand it myself but I intend to find out, I promise. For now, I'm calling off all missions until matters can be dealt with," she told us.

"Could it be because of Lumin?" someone asked.

She stiffens. "Honestly, I don't know." I can tell she evading the question. Later on, I'll demand why. I definitely will.

Lady Hood/ Xelle

This day needed to end. It really does. My crew was disappointed about losing the creds. 350 million creds to be exact. Shit!

Khora

I can't believe that asshole talked to me like that. The nerve. He had better not help my grandfather get that ungrateful bitch of a sister, Xelle, after I've done everything to get rid of her. Why does Grandfather want her back anyway.

I went to my Grandfather's room to see him.

Time to fake the funk, I coached myself.

I walked in and greeted him. "Hello, Grandfather," I said to him.

"Khora, come in and have a seat," he said to me. "We need to talk."

"What about?"

"We are close to finding Xelle..."

Why should I care? "That's great, Grandfather," I lied.

I looked at him and saw he's excited. Innerly, I rolled my eyes. Xelle was always his favorite . I wish that I was. I've always been there not her. Partly my fault but no one knows. That is a beautiful thing.

<u>Lumin</u>

I have Xelle's grandfather eating out the palm of my hands. He's soaking up all the information I gave him. He has stopped every mission I told him about. I have a shit eating grin at how Xelle must be feeling. The rest of the crew will join me soon. I rub my hands together as I laugh evilly.

Chapter 8

<u>Unknown</u>

I have a mission to do. I have to sit here watching this old man until I get the signal to move. I have been waiting eight days going on nine days. I am getting impatient. Really impatient.

I watched and listened to the old man from my van around the corner. Watching the coming and goings was driving me insane. I wanted to call the caller but they always call private.

My phone rings. I looked at it and the number is private as usual. I answer it.

"Hello?" I answered.

"Keegan, the target will be at work until seven tonight," a distorted voice told me. "Make sure to do nothing until I text or call you."

"But..."

Before I could finish my sentence, the unknown private caller hung up.

"Shit!" hanging up the phone.

<u>Kismet</u>

Everyone have been on their toes around Xelle. She has been snapping at everyone. Including Keandre and myself.

Currently, I'm going to see Xelle now. I'm walking towards her office. I knocked on the door and waited.

"What?!" Xelle demanded.

"It's Kismet, Xelle," I told her.

She was quiet for a few seconds. "Come in," she snapped.

I opened the door and walked in.

"Close the door," she said. I do as she says. "What do you want, Kismet?" not looking up from her papers.

"I'm tired of having to walk on tip toes around you," I said, bluntly. "Just because..."

"Kismet..." she sighed.

"No, don't you Kismet me, damn it. You're our leader. Lady Hood, Xelle. You don't want more people leaving, do you? They're already threatening to do so."

She looked up at me after I said the last sentence, I spoke. She put down her papers to rub her temples. "Call a meeting,Kismet," was all she said.

<u>Lady Hood/ Xelle</u>

As everyone filed in, I stood in front of the room. They were slowly quieting down. When they did, I began speaking.

"I apologize for how I have acting and treating you all. Sorry. You shouldn't have had to deal with that. Again, I'm so sorry.

As for us doing the mission, we might have to hold out on that for a while. Our plans has been leaked somehow..." Lumin probably. "I'm trying to make new mission in different location than the one I've had planned."

"When will that be?" Keandre spoke up.

I had no idea he was in the room. I guess I wasn't paying any attention. I should talk to him later.

"I don't know but I have been working hard on it. I promise you," I replied.

"Do you need any help?" Kismet asked. "I'm available. So are the others."

"Thank you but no. Not just yet,' I declined.

Everyone nodded in acceptance. Keandre stayed quiet after the one question he asked.

Definitely have to talk to him later after this.

"Anymore questions or concerns?" I wait a minute before speaking again. "Alright, meeting adjourned. Keandre, please stay back. I need to speak with you." He nodded.

"Ooooh," my crew cooed.

"Bye," I said, joked. "Come see me in my office if you need me."

I walked out leaving Keandre to follow.

Dresden McKade/ Keandre

I followed Xelle out the room. I caught up with her as her she asked through th hall.

"So, what you wanted to speak to me about?" I finally asked.

"Not here," she said. "Follow me. I wanted to speak privately."

I just nodded and said "Okay."

She walked me to an area I never seen before. She then pulled me into a room with her. She shut the door and walked towards me.

"What are you doing?" I asked, stepping back.

She stopped in her tracks. "Nothing, I guess."

"Then explain, what has been going on with you?" folding my arms across my chest.

"After Lumin made his escape, everything went down hill. The mission, half to a third of the crew is gone... it affected my mood. It's like Lumin sold or volunteered the mission to the blue suits or something..." she said.

"Then why evade me, Xelle? Why?" I demanded. "I thought..." I don't know what I thought. I just know I might have feeling for Xelle without even knowing it.

"I know what you, Keandre. I don't know when but I started having feelins for you. I still don't know you well enough or how I feel about that."

I nodded in agreement but stayed quiet. Unknown what to say to her. I understand where she's coming from because I feel the same way.

She continued spoke as she took out a cigarette and lit it. Xelle took a pill and the exhaled.

Scorpius Stone

Two months later, there wasn't any activity from Lady Hood and her crew. Strange. It's almost like... No. No, well maybe.

"Grandfather," Khora called me.

I rolled my eyes. Spoiled brat. "Yes, Khora," I replied.

"It's time for your medicine," she told me, shaking my medicine box.

"Not right now, Khora. I'm busy," I told her.

"Grandfather, it's time to take them. It's getting late."

"Ugh, I said not right now." Will she leave me alone. Nagging wench.

<u>Khora</u>

Ugh. This old geezer. I wish he would take his medication so he would sleep and I can leave. This place smells like cheap cologne and old people. Ew.

I walked to his office and stood in the doorway. Old geezer. "Come on. Time to take your meds. You remember what the doctor said."

"Fine," he gave up. "Leave them there on the desk and leave me be."

Rude. "No, I have to watch you take them."

"Ugh. Fine." he took them and took a sip of water. "Happy now?"

"Ecstatic. Come on let's get you in bed," helping my grandfather up to the his room. That was next to his office. Ugh, so heavy.

<u>Unknown/ Keegen</u>

I haven't heard from the unknown caller for a while. I'm sort of glad bu I still have to monitor my target. After two months, I grew weary of watching them. Day in and day out.

Suddenly, out of the blue, the phone rang and on the third ring I answered.

"Hello?" I answered.

"You will be getting information on your current target. More like more information. I want you to kill the target as soon as possible. Yesterday even," the unknown caller states.

"You got me," then they hung up.

Game on.

An hour later

I drove to my target's last known location. Once there, I get out and sneak into the target's estate. With my gun and silencer, I enter the target's chambers. I saw they was asleep and pointed my gun at them. I cock it as quietly as I could and shot twice. One in the head and the other in the chest, I then left.

<u>Lady Hood/ Xelle</u>

I was working in my office listening to the radio when a broadcast came on.

"Sorry to interrupt your scheduled broadcast. Breaking news..." the announcer said. "There was a homicide shooting of an elderly man. 82 years of age. The CEO of the Dragon Corporation, Scorpius Stone was shoot and killed in his Dorlake home. We will update everyone on the details as we get them. Now, back to your previous scheduled broadcast."

I turned off the radio and sat there in shock. Someone killed Pops and I don't what to do. I continued to sit in shock and awe when someone knocked on the door. I was too shocked to say anything but "Enter."

I heard them open the door and closed it.

"Elle, came as soon as I heard," Kismet said, hugging me tightly. "Are you alright?.. Clearly, you're in shocked. Of course, you are."

I started staring into space. My hearing tunneled. I bared heard her. Only thing I thought about is my Pops, my grandfather, being dead. Who would do this to them? I know he made enemies but shit...

<u>Kismet</u>

Damn it. Who would do this to Xelle's Pops? I should go get Keandre to comfort her or something. But I can't tell Xelle's secret to anyone, let alone him. What am I going to do with her?

Oh, I can just call Nevaeh, the crews doctor. Nevaeh had her medical degree but she got burned out. I let go Xelle to call Dr. Nevaeh answered.

"Hello?" Dr, Nevaeh answered.

"Hey, it's Kismet," I said.

"What can I do for you?" she asked.

"We need you. It's Xelle."

"Shit! Damn it, I heard what happened." I heard rustling. "I'll be there soon."

"Thank you, I'll let the guards know."

"Be there in forty," then hung up.

I walked to the guards station and inform them of Dr. Nevaeh coming to see Xelle.

Thirty minutes later, Dr. Nevaeh, Xelle, and I were together in Xelle's chambers. The doctor is trying to get Xelle out of her shock and immobile state. Many things failed but she didn't give up.

The funny thing is that works is the doctor just smacking Xelle's face. Helping her out of her previous state.

"I could of done that," I snapped, checking Xelle out.

"Ouch!" Xelle exclaimed.

"Why didn't you?" Dr. Nevaeh asked me as she unpacked her things. "I'm going to stick around for a bit to monitor you, Xelle."

"Why? I'm fine," Xelle said, getting up.

We push her down back on the bed.

"No, you're not fine, Elle. Look at what just happened. If someone else would have found you...Keandre? One of the crew? Lumin?"

"I'm happy you found me, Kismet. I really am but I'm fine now," she said, trying to get up again. Only to be pushed down once more. "Come on! Seriously! I'm fine."

"You're not fine, Elle," I said. "Your grandfather was just killed. You need to..."

"I need to work. I need to fix the problem..." she said.

"It can wait. Your grandfather just died," Dr. Nevaeh said. "You need to grieve him, Xelle. Take a while to grieve. Okay?"

Xelle's shoulders dropped as she covers her face. I knew she was crying.

<u>Dresden McKade/ Keandre</u>

Somethings up because Xelle has been absent from the meetings and Kismet is in charge temporarily. I wonder why. Not that I should be worried. The doctor is here which is weird. Never knew they had one.

I should find Xelle to see how she is. I walked towards her office then her chambers when I couldn't find her. Guards blocked my way as I try to go in.

"Sorry, you can't go in there," one of the guards told me.

"Why?" I asked.

"She isn't seeing anyone at the moment. We'll let you know," the other guard informed me.

Puzzled, I walked away.

<u>Unknown/ Keegan</u>

My payment comes through, 3,500 creds is sent to my overseas account. Cool, I'm glad but why an old man? I don't get it. What has that old man do to anyone?

My phone rings again and I answer it.

"Hello?" I answered.

"First, you were sloppy. Second, I gave you half of the money because of that. Thirty, I have another target for you to make up your mistake. I have emailed the name. You find where she is and take care of her," the distorted voice reprimanded me then hung up before I could say anything.

I checked my laptop emails and got my target's name. I then printed it and searched for last know.

Chapter 9

<u>Lady Hood/ Xelle</u>

Two weeks later, I isolated myself from everyone, including Keandre. I have Kismet in charge of everything. Damn, I'm horny. I need to... Before I could finish my thought, I heard the guards sending Keandre away.

No, don't, I wanted to yell but I don't. I heard his feet retreat. Damn.

"So, how are you feeling, Xelle?" Dr. Nevaeh asked, checking me out.

"I'm fine. Just fine," I confessed, somewhat lying.

I can tell that she found it hard to believe me after everything happened. She knew I was putting on a front to get out of here. She eyed me hard and shook her head. Noting my action and lie. She noted a couple of other things before getting up and checking me over again.

A couple of minutes later, Dr. Nevaeh sighed.

"You don't have to lie, Xelle," she said. "I know you're hurting. I heard about Lumin and..."

"Doc, don't. I can't right now. Not not," I countered.

"Yes, now. You aren't leaving here until you spill. Talk to me, Elle. We was always used to talk. Why not now?"

"I'm not ready, okay!" I yelled at her. Tears flowing down my cheeks. "My Pops has been killed by God knows who and Lumin... Lumin is God knows where with a third of my crew. Shit! I hate crying," wiping my eyes. Dr. Nevaeh handed a tissue. I dab my eyes with it.

Dresden McKade/ Keandre

I can't take it any longer. Stopping in mid-stride and turning around. I walked back towards Xelle's chambers. Once outside, I ordered the guards to let me see Xelle or else.

The guards look at each other then at me. One of them knocked on the door. A woman's voice I didn't recognize answered.

"Yes?" she yelled.

"Someone, a man, wants..." the one guard spoke began.

"No, I demand to see Xelle. I thought you were helping her, not whoever had her," I exclaimed.

"He demands to see Xelle," the one guard told the woman.

"Tell him to go aw..." it went silent then. "Tell him to come in."

"You can go in, sir."

"Thanks," I pushed pass them into the room.

I walked into Xelle's chambers. I saw Xelle crying on the bed, a tissue in her hand. I then saw a woman sitting next to her. She looked familiar.

"You look familiar," I said. "Who are you?"

"Doctor Nevaeh Sharpe, nice to meet you..."

"Keandre. Keandre Knight."

"Nice to meet you, Mr. Knight. I was just treating Xelle for cold she had."

I knew was lying, immediately but I let it go. I was lying about my identity. I turned to Xelle and asked.

"Everything, okay?" sitting on the other side of her.

Xelle sniffs. She has never done that before. She was always been strong.

"I'm fine, Keandre," she lied. "Just had a cold. I'm getting better." I just looked at her with doubt. "I'm fine... really. I promise."

Dr. Nevaeh

I hate lying. I can tell this Keandre Knight character knew for a fact is CEO Dresden McKade. What is he even doing here? What's between those two? I'll ask Xelle after he leaves.

<u>Khora</u>

I'm at the morgue. The coroner called me to come in and identity my Grandfather's body. I walked in the viewing area. My husband held me as the pulling back the sheet.

I saw the body of my grandfather laying on the cold slab. I began crying.

"It's him. It's my grandfather. Why have me waiting so long to identity him?" I demanded.

"Honey," my husband started.

"No, I want to know. Right now, damn it," I exclaim.

"So ma'am but we didn't have you as a contact. Only a Ms. Xelle Stone and her phone is disconnected. So, we contacted you," the coroner said.

"I don't understand. Why would you contact my sister? She haven't been connected to the family in years. Lyzel?"

"I know, honey," Lyzel said.

"She was the main contact to call if something happened to him," he told us. "After the investigation and autopsy, your grandfather's body will be released to you. Since you're next of kin."

"I would have thought you have done all that by now," I commented.

"It's still an ongoing investigation. Like I said before he will be released to you afterward."

<u>Kyson</u>

I don't understand why Xelle has been absent from the meeting and Kismet is in charge. Something changed between two weeks ago and now. I need to find out...

My thought was caught off by the other crew members talking about what has been happening lately. I saw Kismet come in and the talking stopped. Strange. Very strange. Suspicious even.

"There will been a meeting in forty minutes in the briefing room," Kismet announced as she read the room.

Before leaving, she grabbed something to eat. Something Xelle would eat. Hm, weird. She stopped near me and whispered. "I'll explain later." She walked away.

<u>Tej</u>

I tried Mr. McKade's phone. He haven't contacted me in three weeks. I have left several messages but no calls or texts were returned.

"Anything?" Senor McKade asked.

"No, sir. Nothing sorry," I said

"Try again!" he commanded.

"I have several times, Senor McKade."

"Damn it!" walking away.

I picked the phone again and dialed the number again.

<u>Dr. Nevaeh</u>

I watched Xelle and Keandre interact. They were in love with each other and they don't even know it. Hell has really frozen over if Xelle Stone and Dresden McKade got together. Wow.

"Doc, can we have a minute?" Keandre requested.

I thought a moment and nodded. "Okay," I replied. "I'll get something to eat," then left the room.

The guards looked at me as I came out of Xelle's chambers. "Let's give them some privacy," I suggested to them. They looked at me strangely briefly then walked away. "Come back in twenty minutes," I called after them.

After the guards left, I heard talking and kissing sounds through the door. I grin. Finally, I'm happy they found each other but Xelle might get angry about Keandre's true identity. Damn, I feel sorry him.

<u>Lady Hood/ Xelle</u>

I began kissing Keandre. I had to hold me off to speak with me. I wasn't having it.

"Sex now, talk later," I said between kisses.

He kissed me deeply as we undressed each other. He laid between my legs, kissing me. He entered me, thrusting forward.

"Ah," we moaned loudly.

Keandre continued to thrust into me, holding my hips as I have my arms and legs around him. He shift ever so slightly and found my spot.

"Shit," I moaned, so loud I scare myself a little. "Right there. Right there," I said, huskily. "Mm."

He continued to thrust into me. Making my orgasm build.

"Ahh," I moaned again.

He kissed me as began to thrust faster and harder.

"Mm," we moaned as we both of our climaxes hit us hard. "Fuck!"

<u>Dresden McKade/Keandre</u>

I lain beside Xelle. We were both breathing heavy.

"I needed that," Xelle sigh in satisfaction. "I really did."

I just chuckled. "I knew you weren't sick..."

"Keandre..."

"No, you don't have to lie to me."

She stayed quiet for a minute. Not sleeping. I turned to her. She had tears running down her face. She wiped them not answering me.

Before I could ask again, Kismet and Dr. Nevaeh walked into the room.

"Time to go, Keandre," Kismet ordered. "Fun times over. Time to get dressed."

I gave in, reaching for my clothes. I put them on as I get up. Kismet handed me my shirt and Dr. Nevaeh handed me my shoes. I put them on.

I left them. The guards chuckled as I went past them. I turned and looked, making them laugh harder. Weird.

<u>Unknown/ Keegan</u>

My new target was no where to be found. Last known was unreliable because of their location wasn't up to date.

My phone rings. "Hello."

"Have you found them yet?" the distorted voice demanded. "You had to have by now."

"That's true but...'

"But nothing find them and kill them. I won't pay you other wise."

"I'm not able to locate them. Their last known is..."

"I don't care. Continue to try and find them," before I could reply, they hung up as usual.

I slam the phone. "Damn it!"

<u>Lyzel</u>

Everything is going according to plan. I hung up the phone.

"Who was that, baby?" a woman asked, kissing on me.

"No one, babe. No one," I said, moving to kiss the woman. "Mm," moving to get up.

"Where are you going?" stopping me from moving.

"I need to go. My wife..."

"Oh her. What about her?"

"She's expecting me home."

"Who cares? She could wait. I want you now."

"Babe, I can't. She's already suspicious about me cheating."

"Ugh! Fuck her. Stay with me."

"Soon, we'll be together and..."

"You've been saying the last..."

"Baby. Baby..." get dressed.

"Fine...you come back... I mean you'll come back, right?'

"Definitely, I will," kissing her soundly.

I got up and went left the bedroom then walked towards the main door. Once outside, I get into my car and drove off.

Once home, I unlocked the front door. All the lights were off. Hm. She must be sleep. Good. I can just go straight to bed.

Before I could make it up the stairs, I heard. *Click*

"Shit!" I cursed. Without turning back, I stopped waking. "How long have you been up?"

"Does it matter. You're just going to accuse me of..."

Accuse you of what? Cheating?!"

"Khora..."

"Don't Khora me," cutting me off. "Damn it, Lyzel! All the things I did for you!" she got up and stormed upstairs. Half way up. "You're sleeping in the spare room," then continued upstairs.

"Damn it!' I swore loudly.

Chapter 10

<u>Lady Hood/ Xelle</u>

Whoo, that was close. Keandre almost found out about my past. I can't let anymore here know except for Dr. Nevaeh and Kismet. Keandre knowing could be in danger since he's new. Still so new.

After Keandre left and well down the hall, Kismet and Dr. Nevaeh looked at me as if I have grown two heads.

"What was that all about?" Kismet demanded.

"What?" I asked.

"You could been..." she yelled at me.

"I know," I said. "I know. Dang it."

"Obviously, you don't. If you did, Keandre wouldn't have asked those questions," Dr. Nevaeh chimed in. "Now would he?"

I drop my head in shame. They're right. I missed up big time. Royally. "Ugh! You're right. I just needed..."

"We know what you needed, Xelle," Kismet said, snidely.

"Don't start, Kismet," I said. "I didn't mean for this to happen."

"Oh really?"

"Yes."

Neither Kismet nor Dr. Nevaeh believed me, I knew. Ugh damn it, I did this to myself.

<u>Khora</u>

The nerve of that man. Not coming home until I called him back. Damn you, Lyzel and that woman you're seeing. I couldn't sleep thinking about them together. Ugh nasty. Just nasty. I thought he was working late. He came home with lipstick on his collar. A shade I don't wear.

Lyzel has had the same lipstick on his clothes since the maids told me and even shown them to me. I should divorce him and be done with it. I don't need him anymore. Grandfather is dead. Someone killed him.

"Ma'am?" a maid called.

"Yes," I called back.

"Mr. Sakens wants to speak with you."

"For what? And why send you?"

"He's in the middle of something."

"What's so important?"

"I don't know, ma'am. He just sent me to go get you."

"Hm...thank you. You may go."

"But..."

"I will be along shortly."

A few minutes later, I walk into Lyzel's bedroom. I knocked on the door. When he didn't answered, I knocked again until I heard a reply.

"What did you want? Are you mad because I called you while you were with your little mistress, girlfriend?" I chuckled.

"Khora..." he moaned in frustration. "Enough, woman!"

"What? What did I say?" continuing to chuckle.

"Just stop! We're separated. We haven't slept in the same bed nor bedroom in three years now."

"So, we have to keep up appearances...."

"Forget appearances, Khora! I want a divorce."

<u>Tej</u>

Damn it, Dresden. You were supposed to call. It's been awhile.

"Tej, locate my son," Senor McKade ordered.

"But Senor... what about..?" I began.

"Forget that! Find my son! Once you find him, informed me immediately. Order my car, while you're at it."

"Senor McKade..."

He walked off not answering. I slam my fist down on my desk. "Damn it." I sent a text to Dresden right quick.

<u>Dresden McKade/ Keandre</u>

Xelle continued to lie to me. Wow. Kismet and Dr. Nevaeh are in on it and who knows who else. Wooow.

I walked back to my chambers. Once inside, I closed and locked the door. I got out my secret cellphone out of its hiding spot. I turned it on and saw several messages. I cursed softly.

Tej: Your father wants your location.

Tej: sir???

Tej: Damn it, Senor McKade is coming to you once I give your location.

Tej: I wish I didn't have to do this to you.

Shit! Why can't my father be patient? I quickly call Tej.

"Hello, sir?" Tej said. "Where have you been?"

"I'm sorry. Something came up and..." I apologized.

"I understand all that but you put me in a weird position that I can't get out of."

"I promised to..."

Before Tej could reply, I heard my father's voice.

"Tej, is that my son?" my father asked from the background.

Damn it. "Hello, Father."

I heard a rustle.

"Jr, where are you? Do we need to call reinforcements?" my father asked me.

"No, Father. I don't need reinforcements."

"I thought I had to because you weren't updating Tej here with anything,"

"I'm sorry, Father," rubbing my temples. "But I'm fine. I will call you soon. When I get a chance."

"No, we're pulling you out. Get your stuff and..."

"Don't care. Get your shit and meet me at the boarder," then a rattle happened.

"I'm sorry, sir," Tej apologized. "I had to listen to Senor McKade."

"But you work for me, Tej."

"I know that, sir, but Senor has been worried. So was I."

"I understand that. First off, how did he find out about all this anyway?"

"Well..."

I sighed. "Know what... never mind," I hang up. I threw my phone after turning it off. "Ugh, damn it."

<u>Unknown/ Keegan</u>

Still haven't found anything on my target. A little birdie told me something though. I just have figured out a time to figure it out. As I thought about everything, my laptop beeps. I looked and saw an email. I opened it and it said something about my target. Interesting. Really interesting.

<u>Lumin</u>

Good Lady Hood has decided to go underground. Leaving me all the creds. So glorious. Oh so glorious. Something finally going wrong for Lady Hood and her crew. She's finally dethroned. Long live the Queen, not. I laughed.

I took my glass and filled it with some beer. As I finish pouring it, Quinlin walked into my office.

"Someone's happy," Quinlin commented. "Sorry to burst your bubble but..."

"No but. You can't burst any of my bubbles," I said, grinning.

"Oh really. A secret source of mine said that Lady Hood has..."

"I don't care about 'Lady Hood' to be honest."

Lady Hood/ Xelle

The next few day later, I slowly was able to get back to work. I was still not interacting with anyone and Kismet was working along side me to lighten the load. I'm most grateful for her.

I avoided Keandre like the plague. I can't deal with him right now. Not after our time together. He haven't pushed me but I saw him around waiting to get me alone. I want him again, I confessed.

Right now, I'm preparing for a mission. I'm sort of looking forward to working with Keandre again. Sadly, we won't be in the van together because I'll be in disguise for one of the mission.

Kismet. Keandre, Kyson, and myself all loaded into the van. Kismet was between Keandre and me. Kyson was driving. We made it to Thundre Park that was near our targets' location. Once Kyson parked, I asked.

"Everyone all set?" I asked. When everyone replied yes. "Good. Let's head out."

<u>Unknown/ Keegan</u>
My phone beeped. I looked at it. It's a text message.

Target is in Thundre Park

That was all it said. I rushed out and got into my car. I drove to that location. A few moment later, I parked and got out. I walked to the nearest building with my duffle bag. I saw someone or two people going into the building across the way.

I bade my time for my target.

<u>Dresden McKade/ Keandre</u>

Currently, I'm the van with Kismet. She was the lookout and I was on the computer. I was inching to ask her: what had happened to Xelle these past few weeks? I didn't though but I was close to asking.

"Keandre," Xelle called over the speaker. "Keandre."

"I'm sorry. What?" I apologized.

"Did you check the alarm systems and cameras. We need access to them."

"No but I'm almost done," as I typed a few keys. "...And done. You're all set."

"Thanks, Keandre."

Lady Hood/ Xelle

Something felt off. I don't know what it is but something was off. I never felt this before. This feeling off... I stopped in my tracks. I can't shake this feeling.

"Kyson," I whispered, to him next to me. I pulled him back.

"Elle, what's wrong?" Kyson asked.

"Somethings wrong. Somethings not right."

"Everything is fine. Nothings wrong . Come on," pulling with him.

"But..."

"But nothing. Kismet is lockout and Dre is on the computers. We're fine. Everything is fine, Elle."

I let myself be dragged along side Kyson. I'm playing a spouse fighting with her husband. As we act everything out, the guards and security is called on us. More like on Kyson. I shook that feeling I was having. Mentally, I tried to continuously shake that feeling.

<u>Kyson</u>

I had a feeling something was off. Xelle just might be right. I hate admitting anything.

"We should abort mission," Xelle suggested.

"Me, too," I agreed.

Twenty minutes later, we're outside away from the building we were just in. We took off our disguises.

Oof.

<u>Kismet</u>

I saw Kyson fall. I tried getting out the van when Keandre got out.

"Stay here and start the van. Keep it running," Keandre ordered, rushing out the back of the van.

"Okay," I said, obediently.

I saw him rush over to Kyson and pick him up. He held Xelle's hand running to the van.

Ping. Ping. Ping. Oof. Shots rang out.

I then saw Xelle's shoulder became wet. I got out and rush over to Xelle. People are running for cover. They just see injured people and blood on both.

I helped an injured Xelle to our van. Another ping sounded as we made it to the opened van doors. Keandre is a head of me with Kyson that was bleeding worse then her.

Once inside the van, I drove us to the complex. In the back, Keandre was holding towels on Kyson's wounds. Xelle was holding a towel on her shoulder.

"Kyson, still with me! Don't go to sleep. Don't fall asleep," Keandre yelled from the back.

Fumbling with my phone as I drove, I called Dr. Nevaeh to come back to the complex with help.

"Why? What happened?" she asked, utterly confused.

"Just meet us there. I'll explain when I get there," I said, urgently.

"Okay, I'll be there."

Chapter 11

<u>Dresden McKade/ Keandre</u>

Dr. Nevaeh met us in the garage with three nurses. They rushed to Xelle and Kyson inside to the medical room. I never knew they had.

They were led in different directions. Kyson was led behind a curtain. His blood soaked his clothes. Packs of blood followed him. Xelle was led behind another curtain. Blood soaked her top.

Dr. Nevaeh scrubbed her hands with medical soap. She turned towards me. "What the hell happened out there?" she demanded.

"Someone shot at us. I don't know who or why?" I replied.

"Who would..."

"I don't know, Doc. They shot from a long distance. We don't know the intended target. Before you ask, I don't know of anyone beefing with them. Other than Lumin."

She nods. Before she could ask anything more, one of the nurses called her.

"Hey Doc, we need help in here!" the nurse yelled.

"Shit!" rushing pass me.

"I'm not done with you."

"I know. Now save my friends."

After she was gone, I went and checked on Xelle. She was unconscious with a nurse working on digging out the bullet in her shoulder.

"Ahh!" her blood curting scream.

"Don't you have painkillers for her?" I asked.

"We do," the nurse answered.

"Then why doesn't she have any?"

"Sir, she doesn't want them."

"What?!"

"For her, she doesn't like being drugged on pain relievers or anything like that."

"Just give them to her . I'll deal with her later."

"Sorry but you're not authorized to tell me what to do."

"Ahh!"

"Do it! Do it now!" I ordered.

"Okay! Okay!" the nurse yelled.

<u>Kismet</u>

I saw the nurses and Dr. Nevaeh working of Kyson. He kept crashing on the table. There was so much blood and gauze everywhere. I'm calling as I saw my cousin like that. I went to retrieve more blood packs for them because Kyson was loosing so much. I could barely see to pick the right blood type but I got it and rushed over to them with it.

Forty minutes later, Kyson was still unconscious but stable. The bullets was removed. He had for four transfusions because he lost so much blood. I sat holding his hand. I hoped he would wake would soon. Dr, Nevaeh walked in to check on his wounds. After she was done, she finally saw me sitting next to him.

"How long have you been sitting there?" she asked, coming around the bed. She checks to see if I'm alright. "Are you alright?" noticing the blood on me.

"I'm fine. Just exhausted. Truly, I'm fine," I reassured her.

"Whose blood is that then?"

"Xelle's blood."

"Okay. Good. Good," nodding. "Speaking of Xelle, she's fine but angry."

"Why?" confused.

"The nurse that was taking care of her, gave her pain relievers."

"What?!...What? Who authorized that?"

"Keandre did."

I left Kyson and the doctor to look for Keandre. Doc called after me. I hear her running after me.

Lady Hood/ Xelle

I'm sitting up on the medical room bed. My shoulder was in a sling. I'm angry because I was just told I was given pain medication without my knowledge. All because of Keandre. Damn it, I don't like them. They make me groggy. I don't like that feeling.

I heard Kismet yelling at Keandre on the other side of my curtain.

<u>Dresden McKade/Keandre</u>

Kismet was yelling at me for giving Xelle painkillers when she needed it. I couldn't see her in pain like that and I told Kismet so.

"You still didn't have authorization for you to tell anyone to do anything, Keandre!" Kismet yelled. "Damn it, Keandre!" she storms away.

I went and checked on Xelle. I went behind the curtain. I saw her turn and glared at me.

"Wait... Kismet has already chewed me out. I don't understand why you don't like painkillers," I cut her off.

"It's because depending on the medication I could of died. I'm allergic to certain pain and other types of meds.," I told him.

"You didn't say anything..."

"It wasn't common knowledge."

I looked at her confused. "I wish I'd known. Otherwise, I wouldn't have told that nurse to give you anything. As I told Kismet, I was worried. You were screaming."

"Next time..."

"Hopefully, there won't be another time..."

"Next time, listen..."

"Okay. Okay. No more pain meds. I get it. I get it."

Before Xelle could speak, Dr. Nevaeh comes into check on her. Or so I thought.

"Keandre, I need to speak with you," she said then left. Leaving to follow.

When I hesitated, Xelle looked at me. "You better go see what she wants. She doesn't like to kept waiting," chuckling as she leaded back.

With that, I followed Dr. Nevaeh out the room to a private room so we could talk.

<u>Dr. Nevaeh</u>

I waited for Keandre to walk inside. Once he was inside, I let him have it.

"Who gave you authorization to command my staff to do anything?!" I demanded.

"Xelle was in pain..." Keandre began to explain.

"Do you understand that she could've died? All because you didn't want to see her in pain. Um hm." She sighed. "I know you mean well or whatever you're doing. Just take it easy on Xelle, Mr. McKade. She been through a lot. And..."

"Please, don't say that name too loud. No one knows who I am. To tell you the truth, I actually came to care for Xelle. No matter what beef I had with her before coming here. Unknown to either of us, someone was listening to our conversation.

<u>Kismet</u>

I went down the hall to the medical room when I heard voices coming from of the rooms. As I get closer to the room, I realized it was Keandre and Dr. Nevaeh was speaking. I hid so neither one could see me.

"...I know you mean well or whatever you're doing. Just take it easy on Xelle, Mr. McKade. She's been through a lot. And..."

I then heard Keandre. "Please, don't call me that too loud. No one knows me by that name..."

I gasped and slowly walk away. I decided on another route to the medical room. Once on that route, I'm still shocked at what just heard. Keandre is really Dresden McKade. Mind blown. Should I tell Xelle? I should tell Xelle.

I made it to the medical room and I saw Keandre already there. Shit! I groaned in frustration. I decided to see how Kyson is doing.

<u>Lady Hood/ Xelle</u>

A week later, I'm released out of the medical room. I'm in my chambers. I noticed that Kismet is acting strangely around Keandre. Right now, we're in the break room. The cook made a buffet worth of food. I sat with Kismet when Keandre walked in and approached us.

Immediately, Kismet got up and left. As she walked passed, she glared at him.

Confused. "What's up with you and Kismet?" I inquired, once he sat down.

Confused by the question. "What do you mean?"

"Kismet is acting sus against you. What happened?"

Still confused. "I didn't do anything to her. I promise you, I didn't."

"Are you sure?"

"Yes."

I nodded. I really needed to find out what was going on.

A few hours later, I was being checked on by Dr. Nevaeh. As she cleans and re wrapped my shoulder, Kismet came in.

"We need to talk," we said in unison.

"Could you give a minute...alone, Doc?" Kismet requested.

"I'm basically already done. I'll just get out of your hair," Dr. Nevaeh told us.

Once she was done, she left and closed the door behind her.

"Why are you acting sus against Keandre? I thought you two were cool," I asked.

"Keandre isn't who he say he is," Kismet began.

"What do you mean?" confused.

"He's impersonating some he's not. I overheard Doc and Keandre talking..."

"What have I told you about eavesdropping, Kis?" cutting her off. "We've talked about this..."

"I know. I know. I have useful information this time... I was just walking by when I heard them talking."

Changing tactics. "What did you hear, exactly?"

"Do you remember the mission that we did a while back? The one at McKade Corp."

Vaguely. We did so many since then. What about them?"

"I overheard Doc call Keandre... 'Mr. McKade,'" she put his name in air quotes.

"You must be mistaken. You must have heard..."

"No, I heard it as clear as day."

"Are you sure?"

Getting angry. "I know what I heard, Xelle. Are you going to do something about it or talk to him about it?"

"Kismet..."

"No, will you speak to Keandre?"

The door opened at that moment. It was Keandre, speak of the devil. I turned to Kismet, who was currently once again glaring at him. She got up to leave. Keandre noticed.

"What's your deal, Kismet?" Keandre demanded.

"You're my deal, Keandre," she responded. "Lying to all of us..."

"What are you talking about?"

Dresden Mckade/ Keandre

"...What are you talking about?" I reiterated, suspiciously. "I haven't lied to anyone."

"Are you sure about you're not to us, Dresden... I mean Keandre?" Kismet said, snidely.

How did she find out. No one knows my true identity but the doctor. The doctor kept her word since we talked and I kept mine.

Before I could reply, someone banged out the door.

"Who is it?!" all of three yelled in unison.

"It's Ms. Teal, ma'am. Dr. Nevaeh asked me to collect you and Ms. Ichirin."

Kismet rushed to the door and opened it. "What's wrong? Is it Kyson?"

"Dr. Nevaeh just asked to go and collect you two, ma'am," Ms. Teal replied.

Kismet followed her. Leaving Xelle me to follow.

Once we all entered, Dr. Nevaeh was waiting on us. She walked over to Kismet and took her hand pulling her to where Kyson lay. Leaving us once again to follow.

"Someone is eager to see you," Doc said, grinning. "Kismet, look whose awake. Demanding to see you."

She walked behind the curtain. I saw her gasp and eyes water. I grinned. Kismet's partner in crime is finally awake.

Chapter 12

<u>Seren</u>

My phone rings and I answered it.

"Hello?"

"Hey Babe," a man's voice greeted me. "Get ready and meet me at our spot."

I hang up then phone and get dressed.

Thirty minutes later, I knock on the hotel door. The door opened and my lover kissed me before pulling me inside.

<u>Khora</u>

After Grandfather's cremation, I was cleaning when the phone rang. *Ring. Ring.*

"Hello?" I answered.

"What the hell happened?!" Xelle demanded.

"So now, you decided to contact the family. I see."

"Cut the shit, Khora! What's going on with Pop's investigation?"

"Why do you care, Xelle? Or is it Lady Hood?"

"Damn it! Just tell me, Khora."

"I don't know what gong on but..."

"But what? Just tell me!"

"If you must know, the blue suits couldn't find any leads as of yet..."

"Okay. So, where is Pop's body, Khora?"

"I had Grandfather's cremated, dear sister."

"You didn't..."

"Oh but I did. It's what he wanted."

"No, that's no what he wanted. You know he would have wanted to be buried next to Nana. You always been selfish."

I hang up on Xelle, was still ranting and raving. "I don't have time for that," I said as I continued to clean.

Lady Hood/ Xelle

I know the old crusty bitch didn't just hang up on me. The nerve. She knew she was wrong. I hung up the phone. Having care with my shoulder, I got up out my office chair. As I walked out the office, I run into Keandre walking pass. Still angry, I saw him.

"What's wrong?" Keandre asked.

"Nothing. I need to find Kismet," I evaded.

" She's with Kyson."

"I got to go, Dre."

"Calm down first," stopping me.

"I got to go, Keandre," I repeated. "I need to talk with Kismet," tried to move past him.

"You can always talk to me, Xelle."

"Dre, I know you mean well but I need Kismet at this point and time," then walked away from him.

I found Kismet walking out the medical room. I stopped her and asked her to follow me to my chambers. She said okay.

Once inside, I closed the door. I'm glad my chambers was sound proof. No one could hear us.

"What's wrong? Why are so angry?" she asked.

"My sister is the problem. Khora won't tell me anything about Pop's investigation and had him cremated," I told her. "Old crusty bitch!"

"Wow, Khora did what?"

"You heard me."

"Wow."

"Yeah."

"So, what are you going to do about it?"

"What can I do? I'm basically in hiding. If I tried to do anything, I'd be caught."

"True. True. But..."

"I just can't..."

<u>Kyson</u>

I woke up with my chest burning. I touched my bandages. Someone stopped me from touching my bandages any further. I turned to see Keandre sitting next to me.

"Where am I?" I asked.

"The medical room. You've been shot. It was fatal," Keandre replied.

"Who..."

"We don't know."

"Was anyone else injured?"

"Xelle..."

"Is she..."

"Xelle was only shot in the shoulder. She has a sling but other that she's fine."

"Oh good. Good."

"How do you feel?"

"Like shit."

"I understand."

"What you mean?"

"You coded four times, Kyson. You was brought back four times, had blood transfusion. You went into a coma all within a week or so. You lost a lot of blood because of your bullet wounds."

"Wounds?"

"Yes, you were shot twice."

"Twice? Who were they after?"

"Like I said before we don't know."

I groaned in frustration. "Damn it! We need to find out and fast."

"I agree."

<u>Dresden McKade/ Keandre</u>

Kyson's right. We need to find out what happened when he and Xelle was shot. There isn't any leads. Kyson and I continued speaking until he falls asleep due to the morphine. I left and went to get some food.

Before I could made it there, I stopped by my chambers. I needed to check ,y messages and to get to the bottom of what caused the shooting. I dialed Tej. He answered on second ring.

"Hey boss," he slurred.

"Tej, are you drunk," I asked.

"Nooo..."

"Tej..."

"Okay. Okay, I am but don't tell Mr. McKade."

"Tej,, I'm him."

Sobering. "Oh sorry, Mr. McKade. How can I help you, sir?"

"Did you hear anything about any shootings?"

I heard him rustling. A chair being pulled then typing.

A few moments later, Tej spoke again.

"There was a few shootings. We have to narrow it down. Give a time stamp," he requested.

"Shooting with a five months," I told him. "Unsolved shooting in the sector. I need it asap, Tej"

"Yes, sir."

"I got to go. Can't talk for long but get me that information. I don't pay you to get drunk."

"Yes, Mr. McKade."

"Bye."

"Bye."

We both hung up. I put my phone away in it's hiding space.

<u>Unknown/ Keegan</u>

Damn it! My target got away. I'm listening to Creed while cleaning my guns. *Ring. Ring.* Interrupting my music. I answered it.

"What the hell was that?" the distorted voice exclaimed. "You were supposed to kill them, Keegan."

"I don't know what happened?"

"I do. I sent an amateur to do a professionals job."

"No, I can do it. I can do it."

"Good because if you don't, I'll have someone take care of you. Got it!" then they hung up.

My music playing once more.

<u>Seren</u>

I woke up alone in bed. I heard the shower going. I got up and went into the bathroom. I saw a shadow figure moving in the shower. Pulling back the curtain, I stepped inside.

Once we were out and dry, he asked for information on my crew.

"All of the crew are standing down. There haven't been any missions since the shootings," I replied.

"Why?" he asked.

"Don't know my boss never said. They're shot."

"I see. Anything else?"

"Not that I know of..."

"Are you sure?"

"Oh wait, you know that guy Keandre I brought into my crew."

"Yeah, what about him?"

"Someone of the crew is acting funny towards him."

"Oh really..."

"Yeah, he was confronted by them with our boss around."

"Really..."

"Yeah really. They then went off leaving Keandre alone with my boss."

"Okay."

We made love once more before I left.

<u>Quinlan</u>

After my lover left, I went to me up with my brother. Once I was at my brother's place, I try and find him. His guard followed me, while was strange. I found him in his office on the phone. I saw me and waved me closer. He ends his call.

"Hey bro," my brother greeted me.

"Hey, what's with the guards?" I asked.

"There was a shooting not far back. I just need to protect us. Mainly you and me."

"I heard that about from our source on the inside."

"How is good old Seren?"

"Lumin, she's good. Still great in bed," chuckling.

"Is that right?" Lumin asked, chuckling with me.

"Yeah, it's right," continuing to chuckle.

"What else have you heard?"

"They halted doing missions once again, also."

"Excellent. Excellent to hear. We don't have to worry about any competition."

<u>Tej</u>

I gathered all the information I could on five months of shootings. Only three stood out. A homicide, a suicide, and an old man being shoot. The third one caught my eye. 82 year old shot in his bed. Two close range bullet wounds. The man's name was Scorpius Stone.

"Lady Hood's grandfather. Holy shit," I said, a loud. I get the information on it.

I typed a little bit more. I saw a sniper shooting dated two weeks ago.

"Mr.McKade might want to know this, also." I wrote it down.

<u>Lady Hood/ Xelle</u>

I went to check on Kyson. I haven't been to see him in a while. I walked to the medical room and saw D. Nevaeh came from seeing him. I stopped her.

"How is he?" I asked.

"Kyson is doing great," she told me. "He actually asking for you."

"Okay."

"Okay, we need to talk but not now."

"Alright."

She left. I walked behind the curtain to see Kyson sitting up.

"Can I come in?" I requested.

"Yes, I want to talk about what happened when we were shot at," he told me.

"What about it?"

"Do you know why they were shooting at us?"

"No, I don't know. Why?"

"It seems like they planned it. Like someone knew we were there..."

"I know but who? Who were they aiming for?"

"It might have been you they were after, Xelle. You do have a lot of enemies."

"True but be that as it may, they don't want the heat that comes with that."

"True, so that why we all gotta stay on point."

"So, how are you feeling?"

"Like shit. What you think? What about your shoulder?"

"Could be better. Still hurts like hell."

We both talked until Kismet took my place. I just member Doc Nevaeh wanted to speak with me. I went in search of her.

Chapter 13

<u>Lady Hood/ Xelle</u>

I find Doc Nevaeh in the break room, drinking tea when I found her. I sat down across from her. She was looking over my and Kyson's charts. I wonder if she noticed "Hey Doc, you wanted to speak with me?" I greeted her.

"Hey Elle, I did," she confirmed.

"What did you want to speak to me about?"

She stood up. "Come with me," then to one of my crew members. "Take care of this, will you?" leaving her mug. She gathered our charts in her arms. She left the break room. Leaving me to follow.

I caught up with her as she enters my office. I entered after her and just out of habit, I closed the door. I went to sit in my chair as I invited her to sit and she did.

"So, what did you want to speak with me about?" I asked.

"I need to head back. I have another client who needs me. I'm leaving one of my nurses to tend to you and Kyson," she informed me. "Don't give them any problems."

"But..."

"You can call if you need me. My client really needs me."

"When are you leaving?"

"As soon as possible. Now, I need to go." I just nodded. "You'll be fine, Xelle."

"Okay."

"Okay," she get up and came to where in sat to hug me goodbye. "Take care of yourself." She let me and leaves.

"I will," watch Doc leave.

<u>Dresden McKade/ Keandre</u>

I saw Xelle and the doctor leave the break room. I was sitting with a few other of the crew, eating and chatting.

"Hey Dre," one of the crew called.

"Yeah," I answered.

"Be careful with Xelle, she has been through a lot."

"I know that."

"No, you don't realize how much she's been through."

"Tell me."

"It's not my story to tell."

"Hm. Okay."

He got up to leave. I followed but went the opposite way in search for Xelle. I found her coming out her office.

"Can I speak with you privately?" I requested.

She looked at me and sighed. "Sure, what's going on? Let's go to a private room."

"Okay. Is it sound proof?"

"Yes."

We entered the private room and she closed the door. She turned to face me.

"What did you want to speak to me about?" Xelle asked.

"The shooting is there any leads?" I asked.

"Not yet..."

"Why? Kyson and the rest of the crew here wants answers. A friend of mine is looking over the shooting..."

Xelle looked at me panicked briefly before she closed the down her emotions to neutral. I noticed.

"What aren't you telling me?

"I could ask you the same thing, Keandre," she countered.

"Was Kismet right? Are you really Dresden McKade?"

"Xelle, we're talking about the shootings, not me."

"Hm," then began to leave.

"I stopped her. "Kismet maybe mistaken about who I am…"

She turned to eye me suspiciously. She nods.

"Okay, I believe you. If you're lying to me, I will put you in the brig and give you the special treatment. Not even your *friend* find you. Got it?"

Sighing inwardly. "I got it."

"Good. As for the shooting I'm looking into it."

I nodded. "Okay."

<u>Lady Hood/ Xelle</u>

Keandre and I both leave the private room. I have a feeling he's lying to me. Why would he lie?

I went in search of Kismet to talk to her about what discoveries I made about Keandre... Dresden... or whatever he's called. I remember Kismet is in visiting with Kyson. I went there for her.

Kismet

"He's who?" my cousin asked, confused.

"Keandre Knight is Dresden McKade," I repeated.

"Come on, Kismet. He doesn't even…"

"But it's true. I heard him tell doc, 'Not to call him that.' No one knows him by that name.'"

"Kismet…"

"Listen to me. I know what I heard, Kyson. My hearing never failing me so, they won't fail me now."

"If you say so."

"I do say so."

"What are you two arguing about?" Xelle asked. We turned to see Xelle walking in.

"Kismet has this strange notion that Dre and McKade are the same person," Kyson told her.

"It might be true, Kyson," she comments.

"So, you believe me, Elle?" Kismet asked.

"Yes, you wouldn't lie to me or be mistaken about anything or anyone," Xelle replied.

"I'm her cousin, Xelle. Kismet has been mistaken before. Remember when…" Kyson began.

"I was five years old. I paid more attention from then on, cousin," I countered.

Unbeknown to us, Keandre was listening to their conversation.

<u>Dresden McKade/ Keandre</u>

Damn it! I should have left when I had the chance. My mission has gotten tricky, now. I must either execute the plan or abort it.

Ring. Ring. I heard rustling. The ringing became louder.

A few seconds later, I heard Xelle.

"Hello?" she answered. "...hold on let me put you on speaker."

A couple of second later, I heard a female nerdy voice that I didn't recognize as Kismet or Xelle or anyone I knew.

"Deena, repeat what just said," Xelle requested.

"You requested information leads pertaining to the phone calls around both shootings..."

What other shooting is she talking about, I thought to myself.

"What was that?" Kismet asked.

"Someone named Keegan was contacted by a Mr. Cisco Sanchez..."Deena replied.

"Isn't that..." Kyson began.

I heard the a clatter of something falling on the tile floor. A second later, I heard Kismet.

"Are you sure? Are you sure it's Cisco Sanchez?" she asked.

"I'm 97% sure Kismet. I'm sorry, Xelle," then I heard the dial tone.

Lady Hood/ Xelle

Cisco Sanchez. I haven't heard that name in four years.

* * * * *

Flashback

I'm in too deep. "I don't know what to do?" I exclaimed. "Ravi, you're bleeding out. What should I do?"

Coughing, he replied. "I'll be fine."

"No, you're not. You're losing too much blood. Let me call my sister for help."

He just nodded.

With bloody hand, I fumble to get my phone out. I dialed my sister number.

"Hello?" she answered.

"Khora, it's me. I need your help," I said panicked.

"What is it now? Are you in jail?"

"Khora..."

"You're in jail, aren't you?"

"No, I'm not in jail. I'm being serious right now. I seriously need your help, Khora."

"What is it then?"

"Ravi has been stabbed. He's bleeding out."

"Oh Ravi, is it? That boy has gotten you into trouble once again."

"Khora, please help us."

"No..."

"No?! What do you mean no?"

"No, I won't help you. Ravi is always getting into trouble. Let him get you two out of it. You're soiling our family name by being associated with that thug."

Before I could reply, she hung up on me. When I looked over at Ravi, he was dead.

"No! No! No! No! Ravi!" I screamed with tears going down my cheeks.

* * * * *

<u>End of Flashback</u>

I hugged myself, shaking uncontrollable.

"Ravi," I whispered.

Cisco Sanchez

Damn it, how could Keegan miss his shot? He supposed to be a top hitman and sniper. How could he miss a slow moving target?

The Stones has go down. Every last one of them must died. My Ravi would be alive if it weren't for that family. I threw my glass against the wall. *Crash.* It shatters into a million pieces.

<u>Keegan</u>

Even though I didn't kill my second target. I have trackers in my bullets. I activated them and search for them with my laptop. I gps my trackers. My tracker lead my target in Sector 17. I began driving.

<u>Kismet</u>

The alarms went off, suddenly. They was loud with a voice message.

"Code 4.5 Intruder Alert. Intruder Alert."

"Damn it!" I cursed.

I saw Keandre rushing in.

"What are you doing here?" I demanded.

"I heard the alarm just like you are." He turned to Xelle. "Xelle, we have to get out of here.

"You're not talking her anywhere, McKade," I exclaimed.

"We don't have time for this. Kismet."

Before she could reply, shots ran out.

"Get down!" he yelled, pulling us down and Kyson off the bed.

We heard footsteps coming into medical room after the guards were shot.

<u>Keegan</u>

I searched behind each bed curtains. My target wasn't there so I left. Before doing so, I heard rustling. Something or someone started making noises. I turned and went back. Going in the direction of it. I then heard shushing sounds. I cock my gun.

"Come out! Come out, where ever you are," I taunted.

No one came out.

"Okay, no one coming out..."

"What do you want?" a woman voice demanded.

"I only want Xelle Stone. Give her to me and I'll leave," trying to be reasonable.

"No..."

"No. No, fine you'll all die."

I started shooting int their direction.

<u>Ezra(Blue Suit)</u>

Over the radio, I heard. *"Shots fired in Sector 17. the Gallos Complex."*

"Shit! That Lady Hood's sector. I drove to that sector after excepting the call. I called for back up.

<u>Nurse #2 Tallen</u>

I came in from getting supplies. I saw blood and injured bodies everywhere. I heard the intruder alerts announced over the speakers. Trying not to panic or be scared, I ran to the medical room.

Once I was close, I saw that the guards were down. I went to one of them.

"Protect Xelle. Here," they handed me his gun. I took it and cocked it.

I turned back and the guard was dead.

I got up and quietly walked into the medical room. I held the gun away from me, stepping softly. Gun shots ran out. The shooter had his gun pointed towards the turned over bed Kyson was in.

I walked in slowly near the shooter. I shot off three rounds. *Bang. Bang. Bang.* With the last shot, the shooter goes down. I walked over and he's badly injured. My nursing instincts kicked in but I had to push them away. I found something to tie him up with. I then found his gun away.

Once that was done, I yelled. "Is everyone alright?"

"Yeah," four voices replied.

Xelle peeked out first. "Is he dead?" she asked.

"No, just injured badly. I tied him up though and I took his gun," I told her.

Kyson's cousin peered out next. "Are you sure?"

"Yes, I'm sure," I said.

Keandre got up, helping Kyson up on the bed after he turned it the right way.

"Are you alright, Kyson?" I asked.

"I'm fine, Tallen."

"Okay, good. What happened?"

"We don't. We got the intruder alert and heard him," Xelle pointing to the shooter. "Shooting. He wanted me."

"Why?"

When Xelle stayed quiet, Keandre answered. "We don't know. I intend to find out," then turned to Kismet and Xelle. "I got to make a phone call." Then he left.

Chapter 14

<u>Ezra</u>

I walked into a bloody shit show. My gun was cocked and loaded ,
I lead my team through then building.

"Intruder Alert. Intruder Alert. Blue suit are in the building. Blue
suits are in the building," was blared over the speaker. "Alert. Alert."

"Shit!" I cursed. "Someone go turn that off," I commanded.

"Yes sir," one of team said then ran off.

"The rest of you break up into teams and check for survivors."

After we broke up into team, my team advanced to the back of the
building. We saw a whole lot of injured and dead bodies. We walked to
a room that looked like a hospital room. We went into the room check
for survivors. I saw a man with a gun in his hands. I raised my gun and
pointed it at him.

"Put the gun down!" I ordered. "Put the gun down, now!"

All five of them froze after the man with the gun placed it down on
the bed next to him. I noticed the injured man on the ground, bleeding
out.

"What happened here?" I asked.

"A hit-man tried to finish the job of killing me," Lady Hood told
me. "Tallen shot and wounded him."

I nodded. "I see," I jerked my head for someone to get the man on
the floor.

They got him up and arrested him. I looked at him.

"Who hired you?" I demanded. When he said nothing, I repeated
the question. "Who hired you?"

"This time he replied with one word. "Lawyer."

"Take him away," I ordered.

Cisco Sanchez

Damn it! I sent an amateur to do a professionals jobs. I called my men in. Five men walked into my living room.

"Sir," they said.

"I need two of you to grab the girl," I said. I pointed to two of them. "Zane, Ryden. You two do it. Bring Lady Hood to me. Now go. If you don't come back with her, you're dead. Got it."

"Yes sir," they said in unison then leaving the room.

"As for the rest of you three, make sure it happens. Get movin'."

"Yes sir," the three man said following after Zane and Ryden.

Hopefully, no errors.

Lady Hood/ Xelle

I can't believe it, Ezra is fucking dog! He's a stinking blue suit! For crying out loud! How couldn't I have known.

"Shit!" I muttered, not realizing that I was being overheard.

"Is there a problem, Lady Hood?" Ezra asked. "Or is it Xelle?"

"Lady Hood to you, you dog!" I exclaimed.

"Well if I'm a dog, I sure got a big bone with this call."

I shook my head in disdain. "Are we done here or are you looking for a doggie treat as well?"

To my surprised, Ezra didn't even flinch at my comment. Unless others who would have gave me the book. It seemed like he wanted to say something important.

"Split it out, Rover!" I snapped.

"Do you know the man that was trying to kill you?" he asked.

"Just some guy. Why?"

"Do you know a Cisco Sanchez?"

"Yeah, why?"

"Sanchez ordered the hit on you."

"Damn it! Cisco Sanchez?!"

"He wants you dead, Xelle."

I began fingering my necklace, thinking.

"What's that?" he pointed at my necklace.

"My necklace? I got it from one of my boyfriends. Why?"

"It symbolizes a truce."

"I know. What's it to you?"

"Does Mr. Sanchez know you have it?"

"No but he will. Here," ripping chain off my neck. I handed it to him.

"What's this for?" taking it.

"Give it Mr. Sanchez. He'll know why."

He waited a little longer.

"You can go now," I said, snotty.

He turned and left.

<u>Dresden McKade/ Keandre</u>

I'm on the phone with Tej. He was informing of the shooting he found.

"Sir, I found one shooting that was closely related to yours. A Mr. Scorpius Stone..." Tej told me.

Did you just say Scorpius Stone?" I asked.

"Yes, I did. Do you know him?"

"He's Xelle's grandfather."

"Holy shit!"

"Tej!"

'What?! That's big, sir."

"I know..."

Before I could finish speaking, there was a hard knocking sound at my door.

"Hang on, Tej," I told my assistant.

"Okay," he said.

I walked over to the door. "What?!"

"Sir, we need to ask you some question," a woman said.

"Why?"

"The shooter and the shooting here today."

I opened the door and I saw two blue suits. They looked at me in shock. They didn't expect me to be there with Lady Hood's crew.

"Mr. Mc..." she began.

"I go by Keandre Knight here."

They nodded. Not understanding why I told them that. "Yes sir," she said.

"It doesn't matter what you go by, what matters is any information you might have on the shooting or shooter, sir, " the other blue suit said.

"Some crazy man came for Lady Hood. He shot at us until one of the nurses, Tallen came in."

"Okay."

"Are there any other questions?"

"No."

"Good," then I slammed the door in their faces. I put the phone back to my ear. "Tej, you there."

"Yeah, boss. I'm here."

"Look up Cisco Sanchez. Any connections to a Ravi Sanchez."

"Who are they?"

" I don't know. You need to find out."

"Yes sir. I will start right on it," then he hung up.

I hung up then put my phone back in its hiding spot. I turned to leave my chambers. I saw a few more blue suits leaving. One of the stood out to me.

It was the man from the club. Freakin' A, Ezra is a freakin' blue suit. Damn it!

Lady Hood/ Xelle

I told Kismet to stay with Tallen and Kyson. I wanted to check on my crew. I leave the room and explored the miss Cisco Sanchez's hitman had done. Damn, I miss Ravi. Tears comes to my eyes at his memory.

"Damn, I miss him," I repeated a loud.

Bloody bodies were everywhere. The metallic smell of blood filled my nose and I became nauseous. It's not like I haven't seen a dead body before. It's just so many of them.

I walked outside to get some air. Mostly all of my guards was either injured or dead. Two men approached me with a fast pace. A chloroform rag hit my nose. I pass out.

<u>Ezra</u>

I drove up to the Mayor's mansion. Security greeted me at the gate. As usual.

"I'm here to see the Mayor," I told them.

"He's busy. Come back later," one of the security guards ordered.

"He's going to want to see," I hold the necklace for them to see.

"Where did you get that?"

"It's for the Mayor to know. Now, let me in."

He picked up the phone and dialed. In whispers tones, he talked to someone. A couple second later, the gate opened and I was let through.

I got out of the car and was escorted to the Mayor. I kept the necklace in my pocket. The guards walked me to the Mayor's living room where he sat with his wife.

"Sir," one of the guards said.

The Mayor looked at him then me. "Honey, can you excuse us?" the Mayor requested. "I have some business to attend to."

"Sure, I'll check on the dinner," she told him. She walked away leaving the Mayor, the guards, and myself alone.

"Come in, Ezra," the Mayor said. "Have a drink."

I walked farther into the room. I sat down across from him. "I can't. I'm on duty."

"Show me the necklace," he commanded.

"Can we speak privately?" I requested.

"No, show me the necklace," he repeated.

I pulled the necklace from my pocket. I show it to him. He reached for it. I hold my hand back.

"Naw," I said.

"Who had the necklace?" he demanded.

"Lady Hood," I replied.

"Vigilante that steals from the rich…"

"Yes her. They was earlier today. You wouldn't know about that, would you?"

"Why would I know about that? After all, she is a lair."

"Why is that?"

"Long story. Now, give me the necklace, Ezra," he ordered. "Or I'll make you give it to me."

"Threatening a suit. How ironic, Uncle?"

"Just give the necklace, boy," with his hand out.

I gave the necklace. He fingered it. "Who did you get this from again?" he asked.

"Lady Hood. Real name is Xelle if I'm not mistaken."

"Is she light-skinned with dimples?"

"Yes. She's sexy, too."

"That's her. I'll be damned."

"So, you know why she gave me this to give to you."

"But..."

"Show yourself out, Ezra," the Mayor said, getting up to leave.

"But..." I got up to follow him but was stopped.

"Bye, Ezra. Leave or you'll be thrown out," exiting the room.

<u>Cisco Sanchez</u>

Xelle Stone is Lady Hood, I'll be damned. My phone rings. I answered it.

"Do you have her?" I asked.

"Yes sir, we have her. What do we do next?"

"Keep her sedated. I'm on my way."

"Yes sir," they then hung up.

I'm ready to go. Two guards drove me to the building where I held people.

Once there, I walked in alone. I went to the room Xelle was in. She sat in a chair. Her arms and legs were tied. A blind fold was over her eyes. She was unconscious. Her head hung low.

"Wake her up," I commanded.

Ryden injected something to wake Xelle up. She gasped and began to cough.

"Take off her blind fold," I then commanded.

He took it off.

"Leave us," I ordered.

"Sir?" Ryden and Zane questioned.

"Leave us," I repeated the order.

They leave. Closing the door behind them.

Once alone, I grabbed a chair and slid it over. I sat in front of her.

"Xelle,, how did you get this?" I asked as I pulled out the necklace out of my pocket. I then show her it. She stubbornly stayed quiet. "You don't want to speak? I see. I'll just call my boys back to have some fun."

"Ravi..." she said.

"What about my son?"

"Ravi gave me the necklace before he was stabbed. He wanted me to have it."

"You're not to speak Ravi's name like that. No matter who you were to him."

"I didn't get him killed. I tried helping him."

"You lie!"

"I'm not lying. He asked me marry him before we were jumped and Ravi was stabbed. We were going to ask for your blessing..."

"If you're not lying, where is your ring?"

"After your blessing, we were going to purchase one."

I let words sink in. Ravi wanted my blessing. I always like Xelle. She was always good to Ravi. Now that she told me what happened, I'm rethinking of killing her.

Chapter 15

<u>Kismet</u>

"Dre, have you seen Xelle?" I asked.

Puzzled. "No. Come to think of it. I haven't of it. I haven't seen her since the blue suits left. With everyone injured or dead, she must have disappeared..."

"Shit! This is bad. Really bad."

"Xelle couldn't have disappeared. Did you check her chambers?" I nodded. "Her office?" I nodded.

"She must have went to get some air. Relax. She's somewhere around here."

"I looked everywhere for her. She's no where to be found, Keandre."

I saw his face when it dawned on him. "Damn it!" he cursed. "If they have her..."

"I know right. Who knows what they're doing to her."

"True. True. Let's continue looking.

<u>Lady Hood/ Xelle</u>

Cisco Sanchez has the necklace. Why am I still here tied up? Ravi's death wasn't my fault. Someone jumped us. I watched Sanchez debating with himself whether to kill me or let me go. I'm hoping for the latter. I want to go home to what's left of my crew. I even want to see Keandre. We still didn't have our talk.

"What are you going to do with me?" I asked. "Just let me go and you won't hear from me ever again. I promise," I pleaded, struggling against my ties.

"Do you know who killed my son, Xelle?" he asked.

"No, they wore masks and they attacked from behind," I replied. "Can you let me go now? Please?"

"I have more questions for you," he said.

"Okay. Can you untie me then? I won't go anywhere. Wherever here is."

I watched him debate on that, also. He paced, thinking. After a while, he took out his pocket knife. "You better not go anywhere."

"I won't. I promise."

Sanchez goes to stand behind me and cut the ties. First, my hands then my feet. I made sure to watch his every move. I knew how talented her was with a knife,, slicing and dicing limbs off.

I went stand up as he move away from me. I stretch a bit. When I was done, I sat back down. "You're not the only one that missing Ravi, Mayor. I miss him everyday. Everyday. For the first week, I was haunted by him day and night. I couldn't sleep or eat. I cried all the time," I told him.

He began to flex his jaw. Tears welling up in his eyes. After a moment, tears silently ran down his cheeks.

"Zane! Ryden!" Sanchez called. They rushed in.

"Sir!" they said.

"Take her back."

"Sir, are you sure?" Ryden asked, puzzled.

Wiping his eyes. "Yes," he said then cleared his throat. "Let her go. Take her to her complex."

Zane looked puzzled as does Ryden. He replied, "Yes sir."

In the car as Zane drove, Ryden kept watching me. Puzzled that Sanchez let me go. Also, wondering why I'm still alive.

"We're here, miss," Zane said, parking outside my complex.

I tried getting out but the door was still locked. "Can I get out?" I requested.

"We'll be watching you, Lady Hood," Ryden told me.

"I would think so. Now, can I go?"

Zane unlocked the door. I got out.

"Nice seeing you boys," I taunted before I closed to the car door.

<u>Dresden McKade/ Keandre</u>

Kismet and I continued to search for Xelle around the complex. I went outside and saw her walking away from a I didn't recognize. The car windows was tented. The car then sped away. Not before I got the licenses plate number.

"Keandre, were you waiting for me?" Xelle joked, walking towards me.

"No, we were looking for you," I said. "Where did you go? Whose car is that?"

"It was no one. I just took a long walk," she replied.

"Why didn't you tell anything to anyone?" I asked.

"I didn't want to bother anyone, Keandre."

"You wouldn't be bothering anyone. I would have gone with you."

"I was fine. No harm done," walking past me.

She's lying to me. I could tell but why? I followed her inside. She examined everything. We walked to her office. A couple minutes later, Kismet came walking in. Worry was on her face until she saw Xelle. She ran over and hugged her. She pulled back.

"Where have you been?" Kismet asked, concerned.

"I went for a walk. A long one," Xelle said. "Sorry to make you worry."

I could tell she still lying. Kismet has a weird look on her face.

"But... but you hate taking long walks, Elle," Kismet said.

"I needed one after today."

"I understand that but..."

"But nothing. I'm fine, the both of you," she reassured us. "Hey, can you give us a minute, Kismet? I need to speak with Keandre alone."

"If you wanted to have sex with him, just say so?" Kismet joked.

"Kismet..."

"I'm going. I'm going," then left.

Once we were alone, Xelle sat down at her desk.

"What did you want to talk to me about?" I asked.

"Nothing. I just hate Kismet worrying about me. You can go if you want to. I'm just going to do some paperwork."

"Are you sure? I've nothing else to do. Maybe I can help."

"Damn," she said. "I can't take it anymore..." pulling the papers down.

"Take what?" I asked.

Lady Hood/ Xelle

I can't believe I said that out loud. I don't trust Keandre that much. There's still the question of his true identity. There's still lies between us. That ends now.

"I need to tell you something, Dre," I told him.
"About what?" he asked.

"About me. I apologize in advance. The things about my life was harsh and surprising."

"Okay..." he said.

I knew he didn't understand but I went on speaking. "I'm Xelle Stone. My grandfather is... I mean was Scorpius Stone. I'm..."

"The billionaire that killed not too long ago. When you..."

"Yes him."

I continued talking about myself and my previous life up until now. There's one thing I'm reluctant to tell him: that I engaged to the Mayor's son, who was now dead.

Once I was done talking, I waited for him to say something. Before Keandre could speak, the door burst open and armed men ran in. With their guns trained on me, I raised my hand. An older version of Keandre walked in.

"Dresden," the older man called, "Are you alright? I heard about the shooting."

"What are doing here, Old Man?" Keandre demanded.

"I heard about the shooting as I said," the older man repeated then turned to me.

"This is all your fault. Almost killing my son."

I turned towards Keandre, I mean Dresden. "You're Senor McKade's son! You lied to me! Kismet and Lumin knew it but I was too blind to see it."

"Yes, I'm sorry. I'm sorry I deceived you," Dresden apologized.

"Let's go, son," the older man said.

"No, I can't. Not yet," he said.

"She tried to steal from you, son. Why are you defending her?"

"Yes, I am."

"Don't tell me falling for the thief. This harlot."

"What if I did? Xelle Stone has been through a lot in this past year alone. More than anyone, Father."

Dresden's father grabbed his arm and pulled him towards the exit. They left arguing with each other. The armed men, also, left. A few minutes later, Kismet came in.

<u>Kismet</u>

I didn't want to tell Xelle I told you. I just went over and hugged her. I felt tears soak my shirt.

"I'm sorry, Elle," I apologized.

She pulled back. "I wish people will stop apologizing... Know what, get out."

"But..."

"Get out. I want to be alone. Thank you."

I leave but not before speaking my piece. "Elle, even though he lied to you, I think he came to care or even love you. I can tell you do," then I left her office.

Dresden McKade

I'm back home. My father's guards was guarding me my every move. I couldn't go anywhere without one of them with me. Going to the bathroom, they're there. Going to the kitchen, they're there. My room, they're there. Can't I have some privacy. I even couldn't make phone calls without them. I couldn't drive myself anywhere because Senor McKade said so.

I'm working going over all I missed. *Ding.* I looked up and there was an email. I clicked on it. It opened up.

Dre,

I understand why you lied to us. Xelle isn't taking it too well.

She stays in her office away from everyone. We need you back.

Kismet

Ps.

I apologize for how I acted. Please, come back.

I read the email a few more times before my father walked in uninvited. I closed out the email as he sat in the seat across from me.

"What do you want, old man?" I demanded.

"Just worried about you. You never worked this much," he replied.

"And whose fault is that? Guards being around me 24/ 7. I can't do anything."

"I have great news," he said not listening to a word it said. "I found a wife for you."

"No."

"No? Are you saying no because of the woman? That thief?"

When I didn't speak, he became angry.

"No, I forbid you from seeing her again," he forbade.

"Calm down, your blood pressure. Xelle Stone is the one I want to be with. I'm too old to have my parents forbid me anything," as I pulled my chair back and stood. I get my things.

"If you leave, don't bother coming back," my father said, angrily.

"So be it."

<u>Lady Hood/ Xelle</u>

I'm in my chambers going over papers. I wasn't in the mood to see anyone. Not even Kismet even though she was my best friend. I can't believe Keandre…I mean Dresden lied about his true identity. I know I lied but in the end I was truthful.

Knock. Knock.

"Who is it?" I demanded.

*Knock. Knock."

"Go away if you aren't going to talk!" I exclaimed.

Knock. Knock.

I pushed back my chair and stomped over to the door. "If you're not going to speak…" I yanked opened the door. "…then go a…" On the other side of the door was Dresden McKade. My Dresden. "What are you doing here?"

"I'm here because I miss you. I love you and Kismet is worried about you," he told me.

"I'm going to kill her," I said.

"Don't who's going to be your…"

"My what?…Wait, you love me?" He nodded, walking towards me. My eyes watering.

"Yes, I do."

"I love you, too." I smiled briefly. "I'm still angry at you."

"That's fine. Just let me stay and continue to apologize to you."

"Okay," I began smiling again.

"By the way, I'm sorry about what happened with Ravi."

My smiled dropped briefly. "Thank you."

I walked over to Dresden and kissed him. I felt him kiss me back.

Epilogue

<u>Xelle McKade</u>

A year or so later

Lady Hood was retired as of a year ago when I became pregnant with little Ravi and Juna. They're turning one very soon. Dresden was playing with them. I smiled as I walked over to them.

"Mommy, play," Ravi said.

"Yes mommy, play," Juna chimed in.

I move closer to Juna and pulled onto my lap. I began tickling her. Juna's giggles filled the air.

A few minutes later, the twins were getting tired. Dresden and I got them ready for bed. They were bathed, changed, and put in their big girl and boy beds. We kiss our sleeping beauties and left the their chambers.

Dresden and I went to ours, closing the door behind us. I'm pulled into his embrace and kissed.

"I love you, Mr. Dresden McKade," I said.

"I love you,too, Lady Hood," he said, kissing me.